# The Kiss that Captured a Billionaire

## HEART & SOUL SERIES

### S.E. SMITH

MONTANA
PUBLISHING

# Acknowledgments

I would like to thank my husband, Steve, for believing in me and being proud enough of me to give me the courage to follow my dream. I would also like to give a special thank you to my sister and best friend, Linda, who not only encouraged me to write, but who also read the manuscript. Also, to my other friends who believe in me: Julie, Jackie, Christel, Sally, Jolanda, Lisa, Laurelle, Debbie, and Narelle. The girls that keep me going!

And a special thanks to Paul Heitsch, David Brenin, Samantha Cook, Suzanne Elise Freeman, PJ Ochlan, Vincent Fallow, L. Sophie Helbig, and Hope Newhouse, Allison River, Jonathan Strait, and Bethanne Reid—the outstanding voices behind my audiobooks!

– S. E. Smith

Contemporary Romance
THE KISS THAT CAPTURED A BILLIONAIRE
*S.E. Smith Signature Romance: Heart & Soul series*
Copyright © 2025 by S.E. Smith
First E-Book Published August 2025
Cover Design by Montana Publishing

Summary: He wasn't looking for love… until one kiss turned his world upside down. Now she's gone—and he'll stop at nothing to bring her back.

ISBN: 978-1-963823-82-0 (eBook)
ISBN: 978-1-963823-83-7 (Amazon Paperback)
ISBN: 978-1-963823-89-9 (BN Paperback)
ISBN: 978-1-963823-84-4 (Hardcover)

Romance I Contemporary I Action/Adventure I Billionaire I International

Published by Montana Publishing, LLC & SE Smith of Florida Inc.
www.sesmithfl.com

# Contents

# *Synopsis*

**Her kiss changed his life forever…**

Greek billionaire Theo Kallistratos isn't looking for love—only a distraction—when he becomes captivated by a mysterious woman sitting alone in his New York nightclub. But when she leaves him with a single kiss that ruins him for anyone else, he knows one thing…

**One kiss will never be enough.**

Rose Smythe is as striking as her name—but she is far from delicate. She has thorns, and she knows how to wield them. Smooth-talking charmers like Theo are exactly what she avoids. Still, their shared kiss lingers… in her thoughts and in her heart.

Theo has two goals in New York: find his godfather's lost granddaughter and the mystery woman whose kiss still haunts him. He never expects both searches to lead to the same woman.

When Rose vanishes, Theo will stop at nothing to find her—but winning her heart is only the beginning. Because loving Rose means surrendering everything he is—body and soul.

Can he break through the thorns guarding her heart and prove they belong together, or will his cursed arrogance destroy the fragile bloom of her love?

# One

**Palermo, Sicily**

The scent of blooming gardenias and citrus drifted through the open doors of the grand palazzo, carried on a cool Mediterranean breeze. Laughter mingled with the delicate clink of champagne flutes and the soft notes of a string quartet playing from a vine-draped terrace. Golden light from wrought-iron sconces spilled across marble floors, casting long shadows, and highlighting the centuries-old grandeur of the Alliata family estate.

Theo Kallistratos adjusted the cuff of his tuxedo jacket, his gaze sweeping over the crowd of European royalty, business moguls, and political heavyweights who filled the opulent ballroom.

Beneath the sophistication pulsed raw power—Sicilian influence wrapped in silk.

His companion for the evening, Allegra Rossi, was striking in crimson silk that clung to every curve. She leaned in with practiced grace.

"Dance with me, Theo," she purred, her fingers lightly brushing his wrist.

He offered a tight smile. "Not right now."

Truthfully, he was relieved when a liveried attendant approached with a discreet bow. "Signor Kallistratos, Don Alliata requests your company in his study."

Theo turned to Allegra. "Excuse me. Lorenzo wants a word."

She huffed, but pasted on a smile. "Tell Papà Alliata I send my love."

As he stepped away, Theo exhaled, loosening the tension in his shoulders. Bringing Allegra had been a mistake. Not because she lacked beauty or poise—far from it—but because lately, her half-sister Gina had been stirring up trouble, and Allegra, in her desire to outshine her sister, had grown more demanding by the day.

Still, when his mother had casually mentioned that Lucinda, Lorenzo's daughter, commented in passing that Allegra didn't have a date for the anniversary party, he'd agreed out of misplaced chivalry—and an even bigger dose of guilt—to escort her.

Now, he regretted it.

The corridor beyond the ballroom was quieter, the air cooler. Ornate frescoes and centuries-old oil paintings lined the hallway, silent witnesses to the history of an Italian dynasty.

A footman opened the carved mahogany door to Lorenzo's private den. Theo stepped into a world of masculine opulence.

Dark wood shelves groaned under the weight of leather-bound tomes and ancient manuscripts. A gilded globe stood near the fireplace, its edges worn from decades of touch.

Italian masterpieces adorned the walls, their moody brushstrokes heavy with legacy. The scent of aged paper, sandalwood, and fine scotch enveloped him.

Lorenzo Alliata stood behind a bar cart, pouring two fingers of whisky into crystal tumblers. At seventy-two, the Don of Palermo retained the stature and presence of a man half his age. His silver hair was neatly combed, his tailored suit immaculate.

"Theo," he said warmly, holding out a glass.

Theo took it with a nod. "Lorenzo. It's unlike you to abandon your own celebration."

Lorenzo chuckled, the sound low and full of history. "Even a Sicilian must take a breath between dances." He raised his glass. "To family."

"To family," Theo echoed.

They settled into leather club chairs near the hearth. The fire had been banked low, casting a gentle glow. Lorenzo studied him with eyes sharp as ever. "How is Alexandros? And your parents?"

Theo smiled. "Good. Alexandros and Dani are happy—expecting their first. My parents are already fighting over who gets to spoil the baby."

Lorenzo blinked in surprise. "I heard Dani is Stuart Bouras's granddaughter."

Theo's mouth quirked. "That was a surprise to all of us."

"They make a beautiful couple—and the merger between Kallistratos and Bouras will be good for business," Lorenzo stated.

Silence settled briefly, broken only by the distant strains of music from the party and the soft crackle of the fire.

Then Lorenzo leaned forward, swirling the amber liquor in his glass. "I need to ask a favor, Theo. One I would prefer remain between us."

Theo's brow furrowed. "Of course. Anything."

"Do you remember Livia?"

Lorenzo paused, his gaze drifting to the flames. Theo stilled. The name drifted through him like smoke—sweet, choking, impossible to hold.

"Yes," Theo replied softly, thinking of Lorenzo's youngest daughter—Lucinda's twin. "She was wild, untamed... a spark in every room she entered."

Lorenzo's expression darkened with old grief. "Her death was... a tragic accident." He took a slow sip of his whisky. "We still grieve her as if it were yesterday."

Theo set his glass down with care. "I know no parent wants to outlive their child. As long as she is in your hearts, she is never truly gone."

Lorenzo looked up, his voice steady but laced with sorrow. "The pain does not lessen, but we have learned to live with it. Now... there may be a part of her that we can still hold. She had a child before she died."

Theo stared, stunned.

"She—?" he started to repeat. "But... Livia was what? Sixteen? Seventeen years old when she died?"

Lorenzo nodded, his expression taut with restrained emotion. "Seventeen and stubborn. Just like me."

Theo sat forward, disbelief tightening in his chest. "Are you sure? You're saying you have a grandchild... and you've only just learned of them now?"

Lorenzo didn't answer with words. Instead, he reached into the inner pocket of his tailored jacket and withdrew a cream-colored envelope. His hands trembled faintly as he passed it to Theo.

"It arrived two weeks ago. No return address. Postmarked from New York."

Theo took the envelope, noting the elegant handwriting on the front— slanted and unmistakably feminine. The paper was smooth, pristine.

He frowned and slid the contents free. There was no letter—only a photograph.

He held his breath.

In the faded image, Livia sat barefoot on a sunlit blanket, her long, black hair wild around her shoulders, her smile radiant and so full of life it made his heart ache. A young man sat beside her, his arm slung around her shoulders, his eyes shining with a proud, jovial expression.

Cradled in Livia's arms was a tiny baby swaddled in a pale, pink blanket. She was holding out one slender arm, and the infant's arm lay alongside it. On each, in the same spot near the inner elbow, was a birthmark—an uncanny shape resembling the Italian peninsula.

Theo swallowed hard.

That birthmark wasn't a coincidence.

He turned the photo over, revealing scribbles on the back. Scrawled in blue ink, almost too faint to see, were the words: Chris and Livia. The infant's name was illegible, lost in a smear of faded ink.

The date: twenty-three years ago.

No last name. No clue who Chris was. Just a moment in time, frozen and haunting.

He looked up slowly. Lorenzo's eyes glistened, glassy with unshed tears, and when he spoke, his voice was raw.

"It's her handwriting, Theo. My Livia's. I'd know it anywhere." He cleared his throat. "Someone mailed that, after all these years... I don't know why, but it doesn't matter. A part of Livia is out there—somewhere—and I need you, I'm asking you, to find her."

Theo's throat felt tight as he stared back down at the photo. The baby —she was beautiful. Dark hair, enormous eyes, a soft, perfect curve to her cheek. A tiny hand curled over Livia's breast.

The sight hit him harder than he expected.

He wasn't one to notice babies. He never thought of them at all, really. But this one tugged at something deep inside him—a protective feeling he didn't understand.

Maybe it was because his brother was about to become a father. Or maybe it was the way Livia and Chris looked—whole and happy, as if nothing in the world could touch them.

"Do you have any idea what her name is?" Theo asked quietly.

"No, that is all I have," Lorenzo said, his voice barely above a whisper. "There was nothing else. No surname. No address. No explanation. Just... this." He gestured toward the photo. "I've had the envelope tested. The only thing we found was the New York postmark. That's all I have. That—and you."

Theo met his godfather's eyes. A man he'd admired all his life. A man who ruled with grace and strength in equal measure, now vulnerable and pleading in a way Theo had never seen before.

"Please, Theo. Use whatever resources you have. Whatever strings you must pull. Just… find her. Bring her home."

Theo nodded slowly, then looked down once more at the image in his hands. Twenty-three years. One photo. A single clue. It wasn't much to go on.

But it was enough.

He lifted his glass, his voice steady. "To family."

Lorenzo touched his glass to Theo's with a quiet clink, then drank deeply.

As the fire crackled softly beside them, Theo felt the weight of something shift inside him—like a door cracking open to a future he'd never seen coming.

~

**The Gerster Theatre, New York City**

The soft crackle of old vinyl drifted from the record player, Ella Fitzgerald's voice wrapping around Rose like her favorite sweater on a chilly day. The basement apartment smelled faintly of lemon oil and cedar—fresh polish layered over memories too old to name.

It had taken her four months, but she'd finally finished. The last of her grandfather's belongings sat neatly folded in a cardboard box marked for the local thrift shop.

She exhaled slowly, a deep, almost reverent breath, and set the last sweater into the box before she pulled it out again and held it against her.

As her hand caressed the worn fabric, a strange calm settled over her, like a gentle exhale from the walls themselves. She would keep this one—her grandfather's favorite.

She glanced around the apartment. It felt quiet now, still in a way that made every creak of the floorboards above feel louder.

The small space, carved into the far corner of The Gerster Theatre's basement, had always felt cozy when her grandfather was alive. Now, with his knickknacks and blueprints and antique tools gone, it felt enormous. The emptiness just reminded her she was all alone.

Her gaze fell on the worn picture frame propped on the end table. She picked it up gently, running her thumb over the image of herself and her grandfather—both grinning, covered in grime, elbow-deep in the guts of a rusted-out lighting panel.

A lump rose in her throat.

Her father had passed away after years in a vegetative state—injuries from before she was even old enough to understand. It had been the death of her grandmother when she was sixteen that had truly devastated her—until four months ago.

After her grandmother's death, it had just been her and her grandfather. He had filled that hole with quiet strength, scratchy flannel hugs, and stories that made the walls echo with laughter.

Losing him had shattered her all over again. The cancer had come fast, brutal and unrelenting. From diagnosis to goodbye, it had been just weeks.

"I miss you, Pop," she whispered, kissing the corner of the photo before gently placing it back on the end table.

She closed the small carry-on suitcase that she had filled with the stuff she wanted to keep. Old photo albums were nestled between a bundle of letters and a faded handkerchief.

A knock at the door startled her out of the moment.

"Come in!" she called, wiping a tear with the sleeve of her oversized hoodie.

The door creaked open, Kerry Evans's pixie-cut curls bounced with her enthusiasm as she poked her head inside.

"Damn, girl! This place looks… spiffy!"

Rose chuckled as she stood and stretched. "It's amazing what happens when you remove thirty years' worth of 'potentially useful junk'."

Kerry stepped in, her eyes scanning the clean shelves, the newly scrubbed wood floors, the vintage light fixtures that now gleamed with polish. "Wow. It looks… huge. You sure you're not just gonna start roller-skating through here?"

Rose laughed, the sound light and genuine. "Don't tempt me."

"Are you staying on at the theatre?"

The smile softened on Rose's face. "Yeah. I think so. I mean… I've got my degree in accounting and economics, so I can work remotely. But this place—this apartment—it's the only home I've known. It still feels like Pop's here. And Mimi hasn't said anything about making changes."

Kerry snorted knowingly. "Mimi would be a fool if she did. You're like the Swiss Army knife of this place. You fix the boilers, rewire the lighting, organize props, patch holes in the stage, and once, I swear I saw you re-upholster a bench during intermission."

Rose grinned. "Longest intermission of my life."

"And in return," Kerry went on dramatically, "you get to live in a charming, itty-bitty basement suite with mysterious plumbing and world-class acoustics every time someone uses the orchestra bathroom."

Rose mock-gasped. "Excuse you—this suite has character. And plumbing that gurgles like a horror soundtrack. Not every apartment in New York can claim such honors."

"Thank goodness," Kerry teased, flopping into the one cushioned chair. "Seriously, though—you've made this place shine."

Rose looked around at the freshly scrubbed walls, the cleaned sconce lights, the polished tile edging that her grandfather insisted had come from Italy in the 1930s. "It's home."

Kerry's tone turned playful again. "Speaking of shining… Wanna go out tonight? Clarissa's new boyfriend knows the bouncer at *The Rocks*. He can get us in—no cover."

Rose raised an eyebrow. "*The Rocks*? As in, that *Rocks*? The one with the velvet rope, overpriced cocktails, and music that'll make my ears bleed by Monday?"

"Exactly!" Kerry grinned. "So… will you come?"

Rose hesitated, arms crossing loosely. "I have an appointment early tomorrow."

Kerry narrowed her eyes. "On a Sunday?"

Rose just smiled, not offering more. She didn't feel like explaining that her 'appointment' involved a graveyard and a bouquet of lilies.

Kerry sighed dramatically. "Please? If you don't come, I'll be stuck as a third wheel, and Clarissa gets mean when she's the only beautiful woman in the group. You know her 'humble goddess' act doesn't last under pressure. I need your sarcasm to shield me."

Rose gave her a look, and Kerry clasped her hands under her chin, eyes wide, lip jutting out in an exaggerated pout.

"Oh, for heaven's sake. Not the puppy face. You know I hate it when you do the puppy face," Rose muttered, groaning. "Okay, I'll go. But only for a couple of hours… and it will have to be after tonight's performance. You know I hate missing them. I need to be here in case something goes wrong."

"Yes! That's alright, we aren't meeting until eleven." Kerry leaped up and hugged her. "Clarissa's boyfriend doesn't get off work until ten. Don't be late, or Clarissa will try to tell the bouncer I'm a stray poodle with a bad haircut and not to let me in."

Rose was still laughing as her friend dashed out the door, calling over her shoulder that she was late for lunch with her latest 'almost-boyfriend'.

Silence settled once more.

Rose looked around her little home—its worn brick walls, exposed piping, the shelves where her grandfather's tools once sat. The clutter was gone, but the warmth remained—and so did the memories.

She reached up and touched the locket around her neck, thumbing the worn edges. Inside was a photo of her parents—one of the few she had —and a tiny pressed clover her grandfather had given her for luck.

"Okay, Pop," she whispered. "I'm doing this."

Grabbing her to-do list from the counter, she slipped out the door into the dim backstage corridor. The old theatre creaked and hummed around her like a living thing.

There were curtain rods to fix, a leaking pipe behind the dressing room, and a flickering stage light that refused to behave.

It was a new chapter, but this was still her stage.

# Two

The low thud of the bass pulsed through the floor like a second heartbeat. Beneath the glass-paneled balcony, the club swarmed with bodies—twisting, grinding, and glowing under violet and amber lights that swept the room like the hands of a restless lover.

*The Rocks* was at capacity again. Downstairs, the bar glittered with rows of glass bottles and flashing cameras. Heat rolled off the crowd like waves, thick with perfume, sweat, and anticipation.

Theo swirled the amber liquid in his crystal tumbler, the drink catching the soft blue lighting of the VIP lounge. From his private booth—tucked into the shadows above the chaos—he observed it all with a detachment that had grown over the past two months.

The music no longer pulsed in his blood. The dancers no longer intrigued him. Tonight, like so many others, he was simply… here. Waiting for someone to dull the tension in his veins.

He was lifting the glass to his lips when a firm slap landed on his shoulder.

"Bro." Nikos slid in beside him with a grin. "Packed house again. Look at that floor—moving like a damn tide. There's a line outside that wraps around the block, waiting to be let in."

Theo grunted, raised an eyebrow, and nodded. "Another great night," he said dryly.

The club—one of three he co-owned with Nikos and Markos Aetos—was thriving. Just like everything else in his portfolio. The investments, the mergers, the acquisitions. All of it was flourishing. Everything—except the one thing that mattered most right now.

Lorenzo's granddaughter.

Nikos leaned back, his arm slung over the back of the leather booth. "So? Any luck with finding Lorenzo's granddaughter?"

Theo set his drink down with a muted clink. "One more dead end. But..." He sighed. "The old woman at the nursing home did give me something. A last name."

Nikos perked up. "Yeah? What was it?"

Theo's jaw ticked. "Smith."

Nikos winced. "Damn. That's practically like saying John Doe. There must be a thousand Chris Smiths in the U.S. alone."

"You think?" Theo muttered, dry as dust.

His fingers flexed around his glass. He owned one of the largest global security and intelligence firms in the world. He protected multi-billion-dollar secrets, governments, and VIPs so high-profile their shadows had NDAs. And yet, it had taken him over two months just to uncover the last name of the man in that photo.

*Fat lot of good that'll do me. I still don't know who he is,* he thought.

He exhaled, low and controlled. Maybe that was worth celebrating.

"What you need," Nikos said, gesturing to the chaos below, "is a little rest and relaxation. Loosen the leash a bit. It's been two months, man. When's the last time you were laid? And Allegra doesn't count."

Theo shuddered. Allegra was on his 'do not touch' list, the same as her half-sister, Gina. He knew if one of the Rossi sisters got their perfectly manicured talons into him, it would be damn near impossible to get them out.

Maybe Nikos had a point. He hadn't been with another woman since he'd ended things with his last mistress in London—a clean, clinical affair, like most of his relationships. But the thought of returning to that kind of arrangement now felt… empty.

Another thing to blame on Alexandros, he mused, thinking of his brother and his newly wedded bliss.

Still, a distraction might help. A brief pause. Something to take the edge off. It had been years since he'd had a one-night stand, but that was all he wanted at the moment.

He leaned forward, his elbow on his knee, and let his gaze drift lazily across the writhing crowd below. His eyes passed over glittering dresses, sky-high heels, and waves of chemically perfected hair. Everything shimmered, sparkled, pouted—until it didn't. Until one woman made it all vanish.

He stiffened, his muscles tensing. A muted curse slipped out as every nerve lit up, like a lightning strike straight to the chest.

At a corner table near the back, slightly tucked behind a column and away from the strobes, sat a woman who didn't belong in the crowd but somehow eclipsed everyone in it. She was dressed in an oversized pullover sweater, worn jeans, and sneakers. Her dark hair was swept into a casually messy ponytail that looked both effortless and… effortlessly sexy.

She wasn't posing, preening, glued to her phone, or clinging to a man. She sat there calmly, a drink in front of her, watching the room with quiet curiosity.

From this distance, he couldn't tell how much makeup she wore, if any. If she *was* wearing any, she was a magician, because she was absolutely breathtaking.

His gaze sharpened when a man approached her. She smiled—politely —and shook her head. He walked away. Another followed, then another. Same outcome. Brief exchange. Dismissed. Her space remained hers alone.

A slow burn lit in Theo's chest. It took him a second to name it.

Possessiveness.

Raw and unfiltered.

It struck without warning. He wanted to stalk down the stairs and plant himself between her and the world. The thought of those men touching her made something dark and primal unfurl inside him.

He had never—*ever*—felt this way about a woman before. Not once. And yet, every cell in his body was coiled, ready to strike.

"You good? You seem a little tense," Nikos asked, sipping his drink.

Theo didn't answer. His eyes remained locked on her. "Who's on the door tonight?"

"Rhys," Nikos replied. "Why?"

Theo lifted a hand, silently signaling the upstairs bouncer. Rhys appeared seconds later, attentive and watchful.

Theo nodded toward the table below. "The woman in the gray sweater, alone. Invite her up."

Rhys glanced once, gave a subtle nod, and disappeared.

Theo stood and watched as Rhys threaded his way through the crowd to the woman. A slow smile curved his lips. There was something about her watching the room with quiet curiosity. She was untouched, real, in a sea of imitation.

Maybe Nikos was right. Maybe a little company was exactly what he needed tonight.

Rose took a slow sip of her ice water and mentally counted the number of ceiling tiles she could see from her angle. Twelve. Possibly thirteen if she squinted past the pulsing LED lights.

She set the glass down with a quiet clink and sighed. "Next time," she muttered, "say no to glitter, body heat, and whatever DJ Sadism is torturing me with. What I wouldn't give for a little Ella or Louie Armstrong right about now."

Her head ached, and her tolerance for over-spritzed strangers had evaporated the minute Kerry had texted:

**So sorry! Called in to work. I owe you. Big.** 🤍🤍🤍

Of course, that message had arrived after Rose was already here—after she'd dolled herself up with lip balm and put on her grandfather's old, oversize sweater that she hadn't had the heart to donate to the thrift store. After tonight's performance of Beauty and the Beast, she just wanted comfort clothes.

She would've bolted immediately if not for Clarissa and her entourage showing up like an obnoxiously perfect perfume commercial: windblown hair, glitzy makeup, and a giggle that could pierce steel. Rod, Clarissa's boyfriend, had brought along some guy whose name Rose didn't catch. Probably something pretentious like 'Bryson' or 'Clifford.'

Apparently, this guy wouldn't be allowed into the club unless he had a date. A 'date' who had rolled her eyes so hard she nearly saw her childhood.

She'd barely said hello before his hand tried to migrate to the region of her butt. That hand had been redirected with a glare cold enough to flash-freeze the surface of the sun.

After that, Clarissa had pouted, Rod had shrugged, and Bryson-Clifford-Whoever had slunk off to try his luck elsewhere. Rose, by unspoken decree, had been dubbed the official table and drink guardian. Which suited her just fine.

No need to fake enthusiasm for the overpriced cocktails or endure Clarissa's giggles weaponized as flirtation. All she had to do was nurse her water, stare at the swirling mass of humanity, and mentally draft tomorrow's grocery list.

*Food. That is something I should have thought about before coming,* she ruefully thought as her stomach grumbled with displeasure.

She stiffened when another would-be Lothario with a dry smile and a raised eyebrow approached her. She offered a sweet smile before addressing him.

"Unless you have snacks, a heating pad for severe menstrual cramps, and a signed apology for the state of modern dating, I'm not interested."

Amusement flashed through her when the guy blinked like a barn-owl, looked confused, and muttered said apology verbally before he wandered off, possibly in search of more alcohol.

She was breathing out another exasperated sigh when the universe decided to level up—or at least double the size—of her next male contender. It took everything inside her not to bang her aching head on the table.

*Kerry is so going to owe me for this one,* she thought, groaning inwardly.

The man beside her looked like a boulder in a tux—massive, muscled, and disturbingly symmetrical. His beard alone probably had its own gym membership.

"Good evening, miss," he said, his voice low and polite. "My name is Rhys. I'm a team member of the club."

Rose smiled back at him. "Good for you. I hope they pay you well—and throw in earplugs and a lifetime supply of ibuprofen."

"I—" He looked confused for a moment before he chuckled and nodded. "Yes, well… um, you've been invited to the VIP lounge, ma'am."

She stared at him. "Why?"

Another flash of confusion swept across his face before he schooled his features again. "Because Mr. Kallistratos requested it personally."

Rose lifted an eyebrow and stared back at poor Rhys until he shifted uncomfortably in his size 16 shoes.

*Who the hell was Mr. Kalli-whatever? A model? A Bond villain? A celebrity from one of those real-life shows that weren't real?* she wondered, unimpressed by the invitation.

"While I appreciate the flattering offer, I'm afraid I'm unavailable. I'm guarding the sacred chalices of my companions." She gestured to the three untouched drinks and Clarissa's sequin-studded purse. "A mission I take great pains to succeed in."

Rhys blinked. "You… what?"

"I said I'm good. But tell Mr. Kalli-whatsit I appreciate the invite," she said, softening her rejection with a sweet smile.

He opened his mouth, then closed it. Then opened it again. Nothing came out.

Rose gave him a sunny smile and an encouraging shooing motion. "Run along now. Go be intimidating somewhere else."

He hesitated, as if waiting for her to change her mind, then gave a slow frown and turned, weaving his way back toward the stairs.

She watched him go, amused, then glanced up—and stiffened.

Behind the smoked-glass railing of the VIP lounge, a man stood watching her.

Tall. Sharp. Effortless in black-on-black tailored perfection. His posture screamed control and confidence, but it was his eyes that made her pulse stutter. Even from here, she felt it. A gaze like flame. Direct. Devouring. Intrigued.

He didn't look away.

*Danger, Rose Smythe!* The warning in her head felt like it was spoken in the exact voice of the 1960s robot from the television series *Lost in Space.*

Rose knew she should look away, but she didn't.

Instead, she lifted her glass, tilted it in mock salute, and took a sip, her eyes never leaving his. Then, just as deliberately, she forced her gaze away and stared at the dance floor like he wasn't even worth a second glance.

But inside?

A shiver of unease rippled down her spine. While her bad side cheered on her false bravo, her good side was shaking its head, asking when she'd learn: *you don't tease the devil and expect him not to notice.*

Her life had been spent sharpening her senses, learning to detect the subtle signs of men like him from afar. She was fortunate to have two master instructors guiding her path.

Her grandmother, despite her petite, four-foot-eleven size, could stare down a street punk or a diva primavera backstage until they whimpered like an overtired puppy. She had also taught her how to discern the subtle tells of deception, even from actors with the most polished performances.

The men here, especially the one upstairs, were the type of men her grandfather had warned her about—powerful, poised, predatory. The kind who saw the world as theirs and took what they wanted without asking.

She fingered the hem of her grandfather's old sweater, feeling his presence, and smoothed her expression. She just needed to remind herself she wasn't anyone's prey. Not tonight. Not ever.

Let him watch.

She wasn't named Rose for nothing. She came with a wall of thorns not even the most charming prince could cut through.

# Three

Rose stood, the thin leather strap of her bag digging into her fingers as she mentally composed her curt exit speech. She had sacrificed enough of her night—and sanity—for friendship and social obligation.

Heavy bass vibrated through her skull, each throb a reminder of the impending man-hours required to clean up the colorful aftermath of the confetti bomb that had exploded during tonight's performance of *Beauty and the Beast*. The Beast's rose petals had burst with enthusiastic vigor courtesy of the special effects department.

She caught movement from the corner of her eye and turned to see Clarissa and Rod gliding back to the table. Clarissa's flushed cheeks and smudged lipstick screamed she'd just scored a VIP pass to her boy-band fantasy.

*Perfect timing.*

She pasted on a smile—the kind that could mean mild concussion or murder in progress—and opened her mouth to offer a graceful exit cloaked in the very real excuse of a splitting headache... when the now-familiar boulder with a beard returned.

"Back so soon?" she asked, her voice dry as bone.

"Ma'am," Rhys greeted with a slightly crooked smile.

Before she could get another word in, Clarissa perked up like a cat spotting a laser dot.

"Hi there, handsome. I'm Clarissa," she purred, conveniently forgetting Rod—who was too busy draining his glass to notice his girlfriend was practically drooling over another man.

*Or maybe that turns them both on,* Rose thought, shuddering at the sudden vision of Clarissa sandwiched between two men. She was going to need bleach for her brain to erase that image.

Rhys was saying something, but Rose was distracted by the shadowed man with the tailored lines and a gaze that burned hotter than the lights overhead. She gritted her teeth and squared her shoulders, sending a silent flare of defiance.

Her mind was already composing a new refusal when Clarissa squealed, gathered her handbag like she'd been personally invited to walk a Milan runway, and beamed at Rhys.

"Come on!" Clarissa said, bouncing in place. "We've been invited to the VIP lounge! I knew this night wasn't going to be a total waste."

Clarissa's gaze flash-burned Rod at the stake before she turned a smile so fake it could qualify as plastic on Rose. It was as if Clarissa thought she was bestowing a royal favor by allowing Rose to tag along.

Rose blinked. "We... wait... what's going on?"

"Mr. Kallistratos has extended the invitation again to join him in the VIP lounge—along with your friends," Rhys repeated, ignoring Clarissa's not-so-subtle excitement.

"Yes! Let's go!" Clarissa trilled. "This is major. You don't just get invited up there unless you're rich, famous, or incredibly lucky. Nobody normal gets in."

"I'm sorry, I can't. I was just leaving," Rose replied. "Congratulations on ascending to Olympus. I'm sure Kerry will love to hear about it at work."

*And try not to trip over your ego on the way up,* she added silently.

"I'm afraid the invitation is only if you also attend," Rhys said with an apologetic smile.

Rose looked at Rhys in disbelief before her eyes flicked upward again. Her teeth ached as the VIP god above lifted his glass—just enough to be smug. She didn't have a clear view of his face thanks to the tinted glass, but she could almost feel his arrogant gaze burning a hole through it.

*That's the Devil, Rose. And you gave him the middle finger. What did you expect?*

Clarissa's eyes narrowed as she leaned in close and hissed in her ear, "You are not bailing. I won't let you sabotage this for me. If you don't go, the invitation's revoked. If it gets revoked, Kerry is going to hear about this!"

Rose hesitated, not wanting Clarissa to make Kerry's life a living hell, but she also wasn't going down without a fight, so she was opening her mouth to say she absolutely didn't give a damn about Clarissa's dream of rubbing elbows with the elite—when she spotted Clifford, aka Wandering Hands McGee, heading her way with two drinks and the confidence only found in frat boys and failed magician acts.

*Damn it. No time.*

With a twist of her lips that didn't even attempt to resemble a smile, she turned back to Rhys.

"Very well." She lifted her water glass like a war banner. "Lead the way, Sir Rhys."

Clarissa squealed again, oblivious to the barely restrained murder in Rose's expression, and tossed her hair, ignoring Rod who was already two sheets to the wind.

As they moved through the crowd, Rose followed with measured steps, fire flickering in her eyes.

*So… Mr. Kallistratos wants my company?*

*Fine.*

*He wants a rose? Let's see how he handles the thorns.*

She was a master of barbs disguised as banter, at sweet smiles hiding sharp teeth.

If he thought she was just another pretty flower at the club, ripe for the picking, he was about to learn the difference between a florist's bouquet and a wild thing grown with wind and grit.

Let him come close.

Let him reach.

Because the next thing Theo Kallistratos was about to learn?

She didn't just prick.

She drew blood.

～

Theo watched from behind the smoked-glass railing, a low hum of satisfaction thrumming through his veins as Rhys led her—the woman who'd hijacked his attention with a single glance—toward the staircase. The crowd below parted, unaware they'd just been rendered irrelevant.

Nikos, slouched beside him at the railing, barked out a laugh. "Did you see Rhys's face? It looked like he was about to be rejected again—politely, but firmly—if not for your lady friend's friends." He clinked his glass against Theo's with a wicked grin. "Good luck. You know I'm going to have to share this with Markos. He'll love it. How the mighty Theo was reduced to blackmail to get a woman."

Theo's lips curled. "Watch and learn. It's about the hunt. A good hunter knows what bait he needs."

"Something tells me you may not want to share that analogy with your lady friend. I have a feeling that little she-cat might just rip your balls off and feed them to you," Nikos retorted with a shake of his head.

"It's time for you to make yourself scarce," Theo responded.

Nikos chuckled again, muttering something about grabbing a drink and working his magic on the Contessa twins—heiresses who seemed to spend more time in the VIP lounge than they did at home.

Theo didn't comment. His focus had zeroed in on the woman below, whose glare—sharp as a switchblade—had sent blood rushing south. That look—pure fire, all challenge—made his pulse kick like a racehorse.

She was the one.

Not the *one* in any fairytale sense. Theo didn't believe in fate, or soulmates, or any of that poetic nonsense. But she was the one tonight —the spark that could make the slow burn of boredom and disillusionment finally ignite into something worth remembering.

She wasn't just beautiful.

She was real.

And she was climbing the stairs.

Rhys appeared at the top a moment later, opening the velvet-draped door to the private lounge. The bottled-blond entered first, swaying slightly, her skin-tight dress clinging to her like cellophane, heels click-clacking with every unsteady step. Theo took one glance and subtly flicked two fingers. One of his bodyguards moved into place, intercepting her trajectory with polite firmness.

The man, her drunken shadow, trailed behind her before he veered off toward the bar like a heat-seeking missile looking for more liquor.

Then she entered.

The noise in the club dimmed, as if the bass itself held its breath.

Theo straightened. Every inch of his six-foot-three body went taut. His gaze swept over her, drinking her in like a man who had never tasted pure, unfiltered glacier water.

She was smaller than he expected—maybe five-foot-three in her worn sneakers—but she radiated a presence that swallowed the room. Her oversized navy sweater slipped off one shoulder, a simple white camisole strap peeking through. Her jeans clung just enough to tease. Her dark hair held hints of red when the light hit it—a subtle halo of auburn warmth that had nothing to do with hair dye.

No makeup. No pretense. Just all woman.

Her eyes locked with his—sapphire, unnaturally vivid, set in a face that didn't belong in a place like this. That face belonged in an art gallery.

*Or under my hands, her head tilted back with her lips parted in breathless surrender.*

Theo stepped forward, unable to stop himself.

Every move she made seemed to challenge him—especially the way she held her water glass like a weapon and gripped the strap of her purse like she might use it to swing at his head if he said the wrong thing.

Good.

He liked danger.

He liked a fight.

He savored the hunt.

He was almost close enough to touch her when she cocked her head and gave him a slow, assessing once-over, her lips curving in mock sweetness.

"Are you finished with your inspection?" she asked, her voice honey-laced steel. "If so, do I get a shiny sticker of approval so I can flash it at the rest of the thousand-and-one guys who tried their luck tonight?"

His mouth twitched. He couldn't help it.

*Game on.*

He offered a small dip of his head, acknowledging her admonishment. The edge of his lips tilted into a smile most women would have melted for. She didn't.

"Theo Kallistratos," he introduced, his voice smooth, low. "At your service."

"Nice," she replied, glancing around the lounge. "Rose. I can see why you like to hide up here. It's much quieter."

His laugh came easily—surprising him. That hadn't happened in a while.

"It is," he admitted. "Although tonight, I'm more interested in… conversation… than in hiding."

She arched an eyebrow. "Is that what they're calling it these days?"

God, she was quick.

He motioned toward the secluded corner booth, a space more intimate than imposing. "May I offer you a seat?"

She looked at him.

Then at the booth.

Then back again.

She gave a brief nod before she sighed and placed a slender hand against her stomach. Her words cracked right through his control.

"Do you guys serve food here? I haven't eaten all day, and I'm starving."

That strange sense of protectiveness surged up inside him. His gaze swept over her again, noting her clothing, the tattered, worn condition of her purse, and finally her shoes—was that duct tape on the heel? His arm immediately lifted when she swayed. His eyes flashed when she stepped back before he could touch her.

"The Club has a world-class chef working in the kitchen," he replied, signaling to a server. "I'll have something brought up. Get me a menu."

"Thank you," she muttered. "I think I'm running on breath mints and attitude."

"You? Attitude? I would never have guessed that from the reply Rhys gave me when I invited you up here the first time," he teased.

"Yeah, well, if he had said you had food, I would have dragged his butt up the stairs and delivered my reply personally. My ribs are talking to my spine at the moment," she replied.

"Easily remedied. Please, have a seat," he said with an amused chuckle.

A woman who admitted she was hungry was a rarity in his world.

He realized this was the second time he had laughed—genuinely laughed—in as many minutes. And with the laughter came a realization. He felt a rush of exhilaration he hadn't felt in years.

This was something special.

He was already addicted to it.

Addicted to her.

He was many things: powerful, ruthless, untouchable—but as he watched the woman with the sharp tongue and the sparkling, defiant eyes take her seat across from him and lift her glass of water like a toast to fate itself...

He knew one thing with absolute certainty.

He was already in over his head.

The table filled slowly—course by course—until it became a miniature feast laid out between them. Theo watched, equal parts fascinated and amused, as the woman with sapphire eyes devoured everything in front of her with unapologetic hunger.

She didn't bother with daintiness. She ate—moaning with pleasure as she sampled the olives, the chicken skewers, the crusty bread dipped in warm herbed oil.

When the truffle flatbread arrived, she murmured something reverent that made his body react as if he'd been sucker-punched in the gut.

He leaned back in the booth, sipping a deep red Syrah, watching her with growing intrigue.

She hadn't given him her last name. He wasn't even sure she had given him her first. He wouldn't put it past her to have made it up.

She hadn't given him much of anything, actually.

Every time he turned a question on her, she redirected it. Cleverly. Effortlessly. With that crooked smile that curled like ribbon around his spine.

"So," he tried again, leaning an elbow on the edge of the booth, "what's a woman like you doing alone in a club like this?"

She paused mid-bite of chicken and stared at him. "I wasn't alone. I came with a group. Granted, they aren't my favorite group. One of them thought a first hello came with butt privileges, and we separated from there."

"If he is still here, I will be happy to have Rhys escort him out," he vowed.

She laughed and shook her head. "Poor Rhys. What did he ever do to you?"

A laugh burst from his chest before he could stop it. "I'm pretty sure Rhys's butt would be safe."

She smiled and shrugged. "Honestly… the person I was supposed to meet was called into work and forgot to tell me until it was too late. I was biding my time as the unofficial table guardian for the sacred drinks of Clarissa the Glitter Queen and Rod the Human Sponge until I could make a strategic escape without damaging my real friend's relationship with said duo."

He nodded, intrigued. "You're loyal."

"No, I'm an idiot for agreeing in the first place," she deadpanned. "There's a difference."

He laughed again—and didn't miss the way her eyes sparkled when she made him do it.

By the time the tiramisu arrived—delicate layers of espresso-soaked sponge and mascarpone—he realized something unsettling.

She'd flipped the entire script on him.

He had been answering the questions.

Not generic small talk. Not safe, curated soundbites.

Real things.

Stories from his family home on Syros. His grandfather's old boat. The time he and Alexandros hotwired a Vespa to get to the local market and ended up being chased by wild goats. His first job in military intelligence. His decision to create the firm.

He'd told her things he had shared with fewer than a handful of people—none of them women.

He was in the middle of recounting how he broke his arm as a teen trying to impress a girl who would later become his first lover, when it hit him.

Hard.

He sat back, his gaze narrowing.

She was good.

Too good.

A flicker of suspicion crept in. Was she a journalist? Paparazzi? Some kind of plant?

The idea unsettled him—but he still wanted her. Desperately. He didn't know what it was about her that made him feel off-kilter, as if he were trying to walk on a surface that wasn't quite solid.

He studied her, watching as she spooned a bite of tiramisu into her mouth with a soft, indulgent moan that nearly drove him insane.

*Focus, Theo.*

He cleared his throat. "What do you do for a living?"

She glanced at him, mid-chew, and shrugged with deliberate casualness. "I'm a bit of a jack-of-all-trades."

He narrowed his eyes. "What does that mean?"

Her smile returned—mischievous, knowing, laced with something deeper he couldn't quite touch. She licked her lips, laughing silently when she noticed him following the movement.

"Do you know what a jack-of-all-trades is?" she asked, lifting her chin.

Before he could respond, she deliberately took another slow bite of her dessert. Parting her lips slightly before she licked them again.

"You missed a spot," he said, his voice low, his gaze flicking to the corner of her mouth.

Her eyes stayed locked on his as she lifted her fingers and touched her lips. "Where?"

He leaned in closer.

"Let me," he murmured.

His hand lifted before he could stop it, brushing lightly along her jaw with his thumb, catching the imaginary speck of cream. Her breath hitched.

So did his.

He didn't move.

Neither did she.

Time seemed to slow around them—the air charged, as if reality itself was holding its breath.

She lifted her fingers to his lips.

"One kiss. You can only have one," she murmured before sliding her hand along his jaw to his nape and meeting him halfway.

Their mouths touched like a match being struck—soft at first, then catching fire.

Her lips were warm and slightly sticky from the tiramisu. She tasted like sweet coffee and sin. He deepened the kiss with aching restraint, his hand sliding to the back of her neck, cradling her like something precious. And it was that lightning strike all over again—only this time, it didn't stop at his chest.

She responded—not shyly, but with a confident curiosity that made his knees tighten beneath the table. Their mouths moved together in perfect sync—exploring, teasing, testing the edges of restraint.

It wasn't just a kiss. It was a detonation.

Everything else faded.

The music. The people. The room.

There was just her. Just this.

And then—chaos.

A shriek.

A crash.

The sharp shatter of glass.

They broke apart just as Clarissa, eyes wild and limbs loose with alcohol, stumbled into the booth and knocked over Theo's wine glass. A crimson arc of Syrah splashed across the front of Rose's sweater.

Rose let out a startled sound, standing abruptly. She snatched a cloth napkin off the table and dabbed furiously at the spreading stain.

"I—I need to rinse this out before it sets," she said, her voice raw with emotion. "Do you have a restroom?"

Theo pointed silently toward the set of private doors just behind the lounge.

She grabbed her handbag, clutching the wine-soaked sweater away from her body, and slipped through the door without another word.

The second it clicked shut, Theo turned.

His fury was instantaneous.

Clarissa was hiccupping something about Rod pushing her. Rod, slack-jawed and glassy-eyed, looked confused—mostly because he was clearly two seconds from unconsciousness.

"Rhys," Theo said, his voice sharp as a blade.

The bouncer appeared instantly.

"Get them out. Now. Flag a taxi. Make sure they don't come back."

Clarissa started to object in a drunken slur. "It wasn't—"

But Rhys had already moved, his massive form blocking her protest. "This way," he said, his tone like concrete poured over steel.

Rod mumbled something as Rhys herded them both toward the stairwell. Clarissa's squeals cut off when the door closed behind them.

A server hurried over to mop the spill, murmuring apologies. Theo barely noticed.

He walked to the railing and gripped it hard, knuckles white.

Below, the dancers moved like ocean waves. Oblivious. Shimmering. Meaningless.

He stared blindly into the crowd, his pulse still pounding from the kiss, from the feel of her mouth yielding and daring all at once.

He ran a hand through his hair, trying to clear the fog in his head. His fingers weren't steady. His body wasn't steady.

He'd kissed dozens of women—maybe more—over his lifetime, but never like that. Never with the world dissolving around him.

Never with the earth shifting beneath his feet.

Damn it, he didn't even know her last name.

Rose—God help him—had just rocked his entire world off its axis with her smile, her laugh, and her kiss.

"One kiss will never be enough," he murmured, stunned and shaken.

# Four

Rose stood over the porcelain sink, her hands working furiously to scrub the deep red stain from her grandfather's sweater. Her fingers were numb from the cold water—she barely noticed. All she could feel —truly feel—was the echo of his mouth against hers.

Her lips still tingled. Her body ached. Every nerve screamed one warning: *Theo Kallistratos was dangerous.*

She wrung the sweater out with a sharp twist, sending droplets of Syrah-tainted water splashing against the basin. Her breath hitched— too loud in the hush of the private restroom—and she braced herself on the edge of the counter, her head bowed, her heart hammering.

*Get a grip, Rose. It was just a kiss!*

That kiss—it had cracked something wide open inside her. Something raw and frightening. She had nothing to compare it to. No string of wild romances, no list of previous lovers, no youthful flings. She was just a smart-mouth maintenance tech with a minor in sarcasm and a major in solitude.

Her reflection stared back at her from the mirror—eyes too wide, lips too swollen, cheeks too flushed against the sweep of dark hair that had fallen from her ponytail. She looked like a woman who'd stepped off a rollercoaster without a safety bar, thrilled and terrified all at once.

"Seriously?" she whispered to herself, her voice ragged. "What are you doing?"

Theo Kallistratos was wealthy, sophisticated, impossibly magnetic—and utterly out of her league.

She, on the other hand, was the theatre's resident jack-of-all-trades. A walking toolbox in sneakers and duct-taped dreams. Sure, she had a shiny new degree in accounting—but her only real-world experience was managing her grandparents' bills and fixing leaky pipes with a wrench too big for her hand.

She shook out the sweater, folded it neatly over one arm, and took a deep breath.

"One kiss," she murmured. "You got your kiss. That's all you needed —right? Now go."

She nodded at herself in the mirror. Go back in. Say thank you. Then walk away. It was late—or early, depending on whether you were Cinderella or the cleanup crew. She had a theatre to clean, a to-do list as long as her arm, and no time to fantasize about a man who collected women the way some people collected selfie images.

Her resolve hardened.

*Disappear, Rose. Just this once, listen to your good side.*

She took one more deep breath before she stepped into the quiet hallway. Her sneakers whispered over the plush carpet. The muffled pulse of the club grew louder with each step until she reached the door to the lounge. She squared her shoulders, drew in one final breath, and pushed it open.

And stopped.

Time crashed to a halt.

There was one sure way to burst any of her fantasy bubbles; and Theo

Kallistratos wasn't just bursting them, he was incinerating them with a freaking flamethrower.

She stared in disbelief at Theo, whose arms were wrapped around a tall, leggy blonde in a skin-tight silver dress that shimmered like molten moonlight.

His hand gripped the small of the woman's back, his mouth locked to hers as if they were fused together. The blonde's fingers were tangled in his dark hair as if she owned him.

Rose couldn't breathe.

The sharp, unmistakable sting of betrayal punched through her chest. She took a step back; the door slipped from her fingers, clicking softly shut behind her.

He hadn't even waited. Not ten minutes.

Her pulse thundered, fury bubbling up—hot and humiliating.

Of course.

Of course a man like Theo didn't mean any of it. Of course he said all the right things, kissed like a god, made her body light up like the Fourth of July… and then moved on—at the speed of light.

*I'm such an idiot.*

Her fists clenched around the damp sweater.

She turned sharply, her breath coming too fast, and spotted the glowing red EXIT sign above a side door. Without hesitation, she darted toward it, wrenching the handle and slipping into the narrow stairwell beyond. It echoed faintly with the pounding of the bass and the throb of her bruised dignity.

She descended fast, taking the steps with practiced ease. Her cheeks burned with equal parts rage and mortification that she could be so stupid.

What had she expected? That he'd fall at her feet? That she, the theatre girl with a stubbornly unruly ponytail and a sarcastic streak, could hold the attention of a man like him?

Hell, no woman could. He was a player, and she'd just been played. It wasn't like she hadn't seen it happen a million times at the theatre when she was growing up.

She shoved open the exit door and burst onto the main floor, the crush of bodies slamming into her like a wall. The club was still pulsing, oblivious to her inner apocalypse.

Head down, she elbowed her way through the mass of limbs and laughter and spilled drinks. Her only thought was escape.

When she finally burst through the front doors, the cool night air hit her like a balm—and so did a broad chest.

"Whoa!" Rhys blinked down at her. "Miss? I thought you were—uh—upstairs?"

She straightened, gripping her damp sweater and willing her voice not to crack. "Change of plans," she said, pasting on a brittle smile. "Tell your boss… to-to have a nice life."

Rhys opened his mouth to respond, confusion flickering in his eyes, but she was already moving—quick steps carrying her away from the pounding bass, the velvet ropes, and the man who had kissed her like she meant something… then shown her that she didn't.

She didn't look back.

She couldn't.

Because if she did, she might cry—and she didn't cry for anyone.

Especially not for the Devil in a tailored suit with a mouth that could undo her world.

Tonight, the rose had drawn blood.

But this time, it was her own.

The Manhattan skyline stretched out before him like a map of broken promises and unreachable answers.

Theo stood at the floor-to-ceiling windows of his penthouse office, hands buried in his pockets, jaw locked so tight it ached. Below, the city moved —chaotic, tireless, oblivious. A sea of yellow cabs, steel canyons, and neon-streaked lives swirled beneath his feet like an ocean of distractions.

And somewhere in that sprawl—hidden behind one of those millions of lights—was her.

Rose.

A woman who'd vanished as completely as if she'd never existed.

He exhaled through his nose, fighting the tightening in his chest. It had been two weeks, and every hour since he'd tasted her, since he'd watched her walk into the restroom, clutching that damn sweater away from her body, only never to return, had been an eternity.

He suspected what had happened the moment he realized she was gone—that she had come back, seen Allegra clinging to him like a desperate barnacle, and drawn the worst conclusion.

And why wouldn't she? The timing had been disastrous.

Allegra had arrived uninvited, sauced on French wine, and launched herself into his arms before he could shove her off. By the time he had disentangled himself, Rose had left.

Rhys had confirmed his suspicions after a search of the restroom to see if Rose was alright turned up nothing. The bouncer asked if everything was alright and told him that the young lady had asked him to tell his boss 'to have a nice life'.

Those first few minutes had nearly brought him to his knees—and he hadn't stopped bracing for impact since.

The realization that he didn't even know her last name, that he could very well never see her again, hit him like a sledgehammer to the chest. Even now, the dull ache continued until he lifted his hand and rubbed at his chest—over his heart.

He turned from the glass with a frustrated growl, raking a hand through his hair. His office was a study in sleek power: black marble floors, minimalist furniture, brushed steel accents, and the soft, perpetual hum of technology always working in the background. Two enormous monitors glowed quietly on the wall behind his desk, running security algorithms and discreet surveillance scans.

Kallistratos Security Systems was one of the best in the world—but none of it had helped.

Finding Rose in New York—without a full name, address, or digital footprint—was like trying to find a diamond in the Sahara.

The office door opened without a knock. He didn't need to look up.

"Nikos," he said flatly.

"Still brooding over Cinderella?" Nikos asked, stepping inside with his usual irreverent energy.

Theo didn't respond.

Nikos took one look at him and sighed. "You're going to give yourself ulcers. Any luck?"

Theo's fingers flexed at his sides. "No. She's not a regular at *The Rocks*. Considering our reputation as a top-tier security firm, we've been unsuccessful far too often lately. We've reached dead ends both in finding Lorenzo's granddaughter and now… now with Rose. Sometimes I wonder if the universe laughs at our misery, Nikos," he murmured, turning to look back out the window again.

Nikos grunted and headed for the sleek espresso bar built into the far wall. "I would agree, but we are tenacious and thrive on this type of challenge. Don't forget that either."

"It's almost like she didn't really exist. She wasn't on the guest list. There was no scanner entry of her ID, no facial recognition trace. Nothing," Theo said in a disgruntled voice.

Nikos poured himself a double and winced. "Right. About that…"

Theo narrowed his eyes. "What?"

Nikos took a sip, then ran a hand down his face. "I was thinking she—

or one of her friends—might have known someone at the door. Someone who let them in—bypassing the club's protocols."

Theo's rage sparked instantly. "Find them. Fire them."

"I already did," Nikos said, meeting his gaze. "But I decided to try a different approach before cleaning house."

Theo's eyebrows rose.

"I threatened to fire them all if I didn't get some cooperation," Nikos said with a dry grin. "And what do you know—it turns out, one of the new bouncers recognized the guy she was with. Rod Turner."

Hope punched through Theo's chest like a battering ram.

Nikos set his coffee down and pulled his phone from his jacket. "I tracked Turner down. He remembered the night—remembered Rose. Didn't know her, though. Said she wasn't with him. She was a last-minute fill-in. He gave me his girlfriend, Clarissa's number."

Theo's pulse roared. "Clarissa knows Rose?"

"Not really," Nikos corrected. "She just met her that night. Said Rose was quiet, but could be a bit of a b—witch. I suspect that Clarissa wasn't happy about being thrown out of the club. Anyway, she said Rose kept to herself. But Clarissa did give me another name—Kerry. That's the woman who invited Rose and knows her."

He held up his hands before Theo could speak. "Don't get too excited. I called Kerry. She was polite for about ten seconds, then shut me down tighter than a bank vault. Said she didn't know what I was talking about and hung up."

Theo muttered a sharp curse and sat down heavily in the chair next to Nikos.

"But," Nikos said, drawing out the word like a showman preparing a trick, "Clarissa did say one more thing—something interesting."

Theo leaned forward, his elbows on his knees, and glared at his friend.

"She said she thought Rose liked to go to the theatre a lot," Nikos continued. "The one near *The Rocks*."

Theo stared at him.

"And?" he asked, biting back the urge to wrestle the rest out of Nikos.

"And," Nikos said, grinning as he reached into his jacket and pulled out a slip of glossy cardstock, "I got us tickets to tonight's show. No guarantees, but maybe—just maybe—we'll get lucky. Or at least find someone there who knows her."

Theo leaned across and took the ticket when Nikos held it out. His heart thudded in his chest as he ran his thumb over the glossy paper.

It wasn't much.

But it was something.

For the first time in two weeks, the vast sprawl of Manhattan felt less like a desert—and more like a map with a single dot of hope. Somewhere out there, Rose was real.

He studied the ticket, his lips curling when he saw the play's name— *Beauty and the Beast*. The irony didn't escape him. She was his beauty, and she probably thought of him as a beast.

He definitely felt like one at the moment—and only Rose could break the curse she had placed on him.

He was going to find her.

No matter what it took.

# Five

The comforting scent of aged velvet and stage paint clung to the air like a delicate, whispered memory.

Rose moved through the wings in silence, her hands brushing the thick ropes that controlled the backstage rigging. The familiar tension in the lines, the quiet creak of pulleys high above the catwalk, the gentle thrum of the building settling around her—it was her kind of symphony.

Soft. Steady. Safe. Unlike life, the stage never surprised her.

She hummed under her breath, the notes of 'Tale as Old as Time' curling around her like a ribbon as she tested the backdrops one last time. The flats slid smoothly into place, each transition as practiced as a breath.

Her hands worked on autopilot, but her mind was stuck in a different time and place. She had done everything she could to push Theo Kallistratos from her mind—to no avail.

She scrubbed and polished floors. Tightened bolts. Adjusted lighting rigs. Painted sets. Balanced the books. Even alphabetized the prop closet—untouched since the 1987 production of *A Midsummer Night's*

*Dream.* Anything to forget the heat of his mouth on hers, the way her body had come alive beneath the weight of his gaze and the feel of his hands.

And still—she felt him. She groaned as the memory rose again with frustrating clarity.

She'd told Kerry everything—every glitter-drenched, wine-stained detail. From the velvet-draped entrance to the moment she opened that damn door and saw Theo Kallistratos wrapped around someone else.

Kerry had been livid. "Clarissa's out," she'd said flatly. "You don't treat people like that. Especially not my best friend."

Rose had tried to laugh it off, but her voice had cracked. Kerry had hugged her tight and promised her a girls' night filled with chocolate, horror movies, and zero billionaires.

But even Kerry's best efforts couldn't erase Theo. She still felt him— phantom touches against her skin.

Rose climbed the ladder to the catwalk, the smell of metal and aging rope mixing with the faint soothing scent of lavender from the rack of costumes steaming in the prep room below. That had been her grandmother's touch. A small, familiar ache settled in her chest at the reminder of her grandparents.

She paused, one hand curled around a frayed rigging line, and let her gaze drift to the stage.

The set was in place—lush, romantic, golden with artificial candlelight. It was Belle's ballroom. A place of transformation. Of love.

A faint smile tugged at her lips.

She closed her eyes and imagined the sweeping dance. Her hand lifted unconsciously, pressing against the small silver locket that always rested in the hollow between her breasts. The metal was warm from her skin.

Her parents had met at a theatre and fallen in love under the spotlight.

According to her grandmother, her father had been playing Romeo to her mother's Juliet—and life had imitated art with heartbreaking precision.

Her mother's family had once threatened to disown her for choosing the stage. Her grandmother had shared that sorrow with a wistful sigh and a disapproving glare every time the subject came up. Her mother had wanted passion, not permission—and found it in a man who loved her until the end. But love hadn't saved them.

Her mother had died instantly in a car crash on a rain-soaked night a month after her birth. Her father had survived in body but not in mind. Five years after he slipped into a coma, he passed away.

Rose had always felt loved. Her father's parents had loved her with every fiber of their being. The theatre became her nursery. Costumes were her dress-up. Stage makeup her crayons. The songs from the musicals her lullaby.

Her grandparents had built a life here, in this very building. Her grandfather had tended to the creaky plumbing, rattling vents, and crafted magical sets. Her grandmother, an accomplished costume designer, had stitched magic into the threads of hundreds of costumes. Many of the costumes were still worn today.

And now… it was her turn to keep the lights on.

She looked across the quiet, empty stage.

In her mind, she stepped under the spotlight, wearing Belle's golden gown. Spinning. Laughing. Reaching.

And across from her…

Theo.

Not the billionaire.

Not the club owner or the devil in a tailored suit.

Just the man. With shadowed eyes and a kiss that had undone her.

Her smile turned wry.

He was still the Beast, she thought, her fingers tightening around the locket. All brooding edges and guarded charm. But in her heart, she had wanted him to be more. She had wanted him to choose her.

Foolish girl. She knew better.

Magic was just an illusion.

Still… what would it have been like if he had meant what he said?

She descended the catwalk with ease, stepped to center stage, her sneakers silent on the wooden floor, and twirled once beneath the ghost of a spotlight. Her laugh was soft and sad.

"Some dreams," she whispered, "are only meant for the stage."

And with that, she turned back toward the wings, humming Belle's melody as the velvet curtain of memory fell and she picked up her broom, returning to the quiet rhythm of work.

The theatre spread out before him like a temple of shadows and glittering light.

Theo stepped into the private balcony box, the hush of velvet curtains and polished brass swallowing the sound of the bustling world outside. The usher nodded respectfully and gestured to his and Nikos' reserved seats—plush, high-backed chairs nestled in a secluded corner of the upper balcony. It offered an unobstructed view of the stage, the orchestra pit, and the layered crescents of seating fanning out like a half-moon below.

Theo had been in hundreds of theatres across the globe. Paris. London. Athens. Dubai. Lavish venues dripping with opulence. But this one— small, weathered, intimate—felt alive.

He sank into his seat, his fingers tightening around the curved polished oak armrest. It wasn't the stage that held his interest, though the set design was a masterpiece of theatrical illusion. Golden candelabras twinkled like stars. The ballroom shimmered with the promise of magic. No, it was what surrounded it—the unseen clockwork of movement—that captured his attention.

Above him, quiet figures moved with the grace of shadow puppets across a network of catwalks, adjusting lights, fine-tuning sound. From the wings, silhouettes disappeared behind thick velvet curtains, guiding actors into place and wrangling props with practiced precision. Every movement was a cog in an invisible machine, orchestrated to bring a story to life.

He was used to watching the performance. This was the first time he truly paid attention to the wonder of what existed behind the illusion.

A soft voice broke his focus. "May I offer you a beverage, gentlemen?"

A young server stood slightly behind them, clipboard in hand. Nikos smiled lazily and ordered a whiskey. Theo murmured, "Bourbon. Neat."

The woman nodded and disappeared. Theo's eyes drifted once more across the tiers of seats. People were filtering in now—laughing, finding their places, flipping through playbills. Anticipation buzzed faintly in the air.

He caught movement below as ushers in crisp black-and-whites guided guests to their seats. His mind, however, remained occupied by one thought. One face.

Rose.

The name was a drumbeat in his chest. A prayer. A promise. Would she be here? Would he see her? Could he get to her before she disappeared again?

When the server returned, she placed the drinks on a small side table with a quiet flourish, along with a crisp ivory envelope. Theo's fingers closed around it. He opened it swiftly, scanned the note, and released a low breath of satisfaction.

He passed the card to Nikos, whose eyes danced as he read.

"VIP invitation to the post-show cast party," Nikos said with a grin. "Nice move."

Theo allowed a rare smile to tug at the corner of his mouth. "We'll see if it pays off."

Nikos clinked his glass against Theo's. "To chasing fairy tales."

But Theo wasn't drinking. His eyes were scanning the upper levels, sweeping over balconies, stairwells, and elevated walkways.

The house lights dimmed. The music swelled.

The play began.

Theo's attention roamed restlessly from the lower level to the upper tier. Searching, waiting, hoping to see a familiar form.

He sat forward, his gaze riveted on the movement high above the audience—on the catwalks where technicians adjusted spotlights and stage cables as if they were playing harp strings.

And then—

A delicate figure stepped into the dim light.

Slim. Small. Hair pulled back in a simple ponytail. Dark jeans. A worn sweatshirt.

His heart slammed against his ribs.

*Rose.*

Awareness struck him as surely as one of Cupid's arrows. His heart rate increased, and adrenaline fired his blood.

She moved with the same graceful awareness, her hand resting lightly on the railing of the catwalk, her head tilted as she scanned the theatre below.

He couldn't breathe.

Then she turned.

And their eyes locked.

The heat rushing through him exploded with the force of a major eruption. The world stilled. Music, lights, crowd—all gone. There was only her.

He saw it—the recognition in her eyes. The way they widened in disbelief, then darkened with dismay.

Her lips parted—and then she was gone.

She spun back into the shadows like an apparition, vanishing behind a column and out of sight.

Theo was already rising to his feet.

Nikos startled, his mouth open. "Theo—?"

He didn't answer. His mind had already mapped the corridor above, the narrow stairs he'd seen near the vestibule. He bolted from the box, his heart racing, his adrenaline roaring through his veins like a jet engine.

She was here.

He tore down the corridor, rounding a corner. A crimson velvet rope marked a narrow stairwell, an aged brass sign hanging beside it:

EMPLOYEES ONLY. DO NOT ENTER.

He didn't hesitate.

He unhooked the rope, slipped past, and refastened it behind him with a quiet click—one more illusion maintained.

The staircase was tight and steep, built for crew, built to be unseen. It wound upward between aged brick and thick beams. The air grew warmer, filled with the scent of dust, paint, and aging wood. The throb of the stage below grew distant, like a heartbeat muffled by time.

He climbed faster, his muscles coiling with the memory of her scent, her voice, her lips.

Their kiss.

She had run from him.

But this time—he would catch her.

The stairwell narrowed as he climbed, the worn wooden steps groaning faintly beneath his shoes. Dust motes floated in the sliver of light from a grated vent, catching on the dark wool of his coat as the air shifted around him.

He rounded a turn, his hand brushing the brick wall—and stopped.

She was there.

Halfway down the staircase, framed in light from an open door above, her silhouette paused. One foot hovered above the next step, frozen mid-motion, as if her entire body had locked.

Their eyes met.

The impact was instant.

Theo felt the breath slam from his chest.

Her eyes—God, those eyes—dark sapphire and brimming with everything she hadn't said two weeks ago. Hurt. Surprise. And vulnerability so raw it twisted something deep in his gut.

For a second, neither of them moved. Neither of them spoke.

He could hear her breath, quick and shallow. Could see her knuckles go white where she gripped the stair rail. She lowered her eyelashes, concealing her emotions, shielding them behind a mask of calm.

He didn't like that. He didn't like to see any part of her hidden away from him.

She tried to retreat, but he'd already seen what he needed to know— that fraction of a second of awareness, desire… need. She had been as affected by him as he had been by her.

He took a step up, slow, cautious, as if he were approaching a wounded animal. He continued until they were level—nearly eye-to-eye. The narrow stairwell left no room for posturing, no place to hide.

She lifted her chin.

"You're not supposed to be here," she said in a low voice that was cool and composed. "This area is for employees only."

He didn't answer.

He couldn't.

All he could think about was the shape of her mouth. The taste of her kiss. The way the world had narrowed to a single breathless moment—and then fractured.

He swallowed and searched her face. "I had to see you again."

Her eyes flickered with emotion again before she shrugged.

"Well, you've seen me. I guess you can check that off your to-do list. You need to return to your seat. Only authorized personnel—which you aren't—are allowed in this area, for safety," she said, shifting up a step.

He reached out—gently—and cupped her hand.

He didn't tighten his grip.

But his touch was enough to make her pause.

"I'm sorry," he said, his voice low and rough. "About that night. About what you saw."

She said nothing. She didn't deny that she had witnessed Allegra kissing him.

"Allegra's an old friend of my family," he continued. "She caught me off guard. I didn't want or invite her kiss."

Something flickered behind her eyelashes. Doubt. Hope. Confusion.

She tried to pull her hand free, but his thumb stroked softly across her knuckles, and she stilled.

"It doesn't matter," she said finally, looking away. "You kissed me. You kissed her. I'm sure you've kissed a lot of women. It was just a kiss. One kiss. Not a big deal."

"It was—for me," he said, lifting his free hand and letting it hover by her cheek before his fingers traced the curve of her jaw, the soft angle of her face. "It mattered."

She shook her head, but he could see the tremble in her lips. "Be real. You don't even know me."

"I know what I felt. I know what I still feel. And I know you felt it too. I want you. You want me."

Her eyes snapped to his, wide and luminous.

She pursed her lips. "Go find another Cinderella to charm. I'm not interested."

She pulled her hand free and started to turn. He climbed a step.

"I can prove it," he said.

She hesitated and turned to look at him with an incredulous expression. "How? I didn't leave a glass slipper behind."

"Let me kiss you again," he murmured, his voice low, seductive. "You'll know."

She inhaled sharply and pressed herself back against the wall. Her hand rose to press against his chest. Her shoulders were rigid, but her fingers curled into his shirt.

"No," she said, her chin lifting and tilting with defiance. "You're not— this isn't—" She bit her lip. "Go find someone else. I'm not interested. I've got better things to do with my life."

He stepped closer, his body taut with restraint. "Liar. Do you think I can't see the way you react to me? This isn't something either of us can ignore, Rose. Tell me that you haven't thought about our kiss over the last two weeks. Look me in the eye and tell me you haven't wondered what it would be like to kiss again."

"I gave you one kiss," she said, barely audible. "That's all. I'm not in your league, Theo. I don't even want to try. Just… go away and forget about me. It was a mistake."

The words hit like a fist, but he understood. She was scared. She might not want to admit it—might not even realize it—but she was afraid that he might hurt her.

He couldn't help but wonder if some other man had. The thought made him want to break whomever it may have been—and protect her from it ever happening again.

Before he could respond, the soft thud of shoes echoed on the steps behind him.

"Hey—uh—sir?" a voice called nervously.

Theo turned, his jaw tight.

A lanky young man wearing a theatre staff lanyard stood frozen two steps down, his eyes wide. "This area is off-limits to patrons. I'm gonna have to ask—"

The look Theo gave him wasn't angry, but it had enough steel to turn the last half of the sentence into a garbled mumble.

"R-right. I mean. Sorry. Uh. It's just..." the man trailed off.

Theo turned back—but the stairwell above him was empty.

She had fled again.

A soft curse fell from his lips as his hands curled into fists at his sides. She was a ghost—slipping through his fingers again. But this time, she hadn't vanished into the unknown. This time, he knew where she was and he would be the one doing the haunting.

He pushed past the volunteer with a clipped, "She works here, doesn't she?"

The guy blinked with a confused expression. "I—I think so. I don't know her name. I'm just a volunteer. Sorry, man."

Theo gave a tight nod and descended the stairs, emerging into the lobby with barely contained frustration burning in his chest.

The curtain had just fallen when he returned to his seat. The crowd stood in applause, the final scene of the play echoing faintly in his ears as he stepped through the private door.

Nikos rose from his seat, his eyebrows raised. "Well? Did you find her?"

Theo nodded once, his voice a rasp. "She works for the theatre."

Nikos smiled, a slow grin spreading. "Then what's next?"

Theo picked up his bourbon, downed the last sip in one smooth swallow, and let the burn settle.

"We go to the after-party," he said, eyes locked on the stage curtain.

# Six

A celebratory hum filled the foyer, underscored by show tunes and the scent of champagne and fresh florals. The wrap party was bittersweet —part wake, part rebirth.

After nearly two years, the final curtain had fallen on *Beauty and the Beast*. The cast and upper echelon of the crew mingled in sequins and tuxedos beside the theatre's directors and wealthy patrons.

Behind the scenes, the lesser cast and the crew toasted each other with bittersweet laughter and hopeful eyes as they eyed the wealthy patrons, hoping those in attendance could be wooed into funding more performances—and the theatre—as they struggled to keep their dreams alive for another year.

Rose balanced the tray of hors d'oeuvres in one hand, moving with practiced ease between the clusters of people, silently nodding greetings and offering smiles. She wore simple black slacks and a crisp button-down white shirt— standard server fare—but inside, her heart beat anything but standard.

A knot formed in her chest as she passed a massive golden candelabra —one of her grandfather's creations—rising like a monument near the edge of the room. She was here to serve, not celebrate. Still, this stage had always been her home. And even in the background, she felt its heartbeat.

In three months, a new production would take the stage—if the patrons opened their wallets. Rose had already seen the rehearsal schedule and production notes for the upcoming production—*Hamilton.*

It was electric. Fast. Unapologetically fierce. A new beginning. She needed that right now.

Rose inhaled deeply through her nose, then exhaled slowly as she scanned the room.

He might be here.

*No, he will be here,* she thought with a sigh.

She'd overheard Mimi crowing about Theo's arrival—and pretended not to hear, just as she'd pretended her hands hadn't shaken for ten minutes after the stairwell encounter.

*Pull it together, Rose. It was one kiss. His declaration on the stairwell meant nothing. He was just giving you a line. You are nothing but a game to him. You tweaked his nose. Men like him don't like to lose.*

Her heart twisted, because part of her wanted to believe him. But logic —that pesky survival instinct—warned her not to.

Rich men don't chase backstage nobodies. Especially ones who run out on them. Twice.

She readjusted the tray, focusing on balance, angles, and crab cakes.

Halfway through the room, she felt the shift.

Like the air had suddenly been disturbed by a cosmic force.

She didn't have to look. She felt him.

Theo Kallistratos had arrived.

Against her better judgment, her eyes lifted—and locked with his.

He stood at the entrance, breathtaking in black. Crisp open-collared shirt. Tailored blazer. The faintest curve to his lips, as if he already knew her pulse had doubled.

*Damn him.*

She dropped her gaze instantly, pivoting toward the opposite corner of the room. If she could just keep moving, maybe—

"Oh, Theo!" Mimi gushed, throwing her arms open like a Broadway curtain.

Rose bit back a snort as she watched Mimi attach herself to Theo with all the grace of a star-struck octopus.

He smiled politely, nodding at whatever she was saying, but Rose saw it—the subtle tilt of his head, the restless flick of his gaze. He was scanning the crowd—for her.

A smug sense of exhilaration ran through her. She wasn't going to make it easy.

Dodging him became her private mission. Each time their eyes met, she vanished.

Until—

"Excuse me," came a warm, male voice.

Rose turned—and nearly collided with a man who looked vaguely familiar. Tall. Broad shoulders. Rugged jawline. A glint of mischief in his dark eyes.

"Do I know you?" She almost winced at the classic cliché.

He chuckled at the line. "I'm impressed. I would have thought you would have been too distracted to notice anyone other than Theo."

"Yeah... and no," she replied with a sense of unease. "What makes you think he distracts me?"

"Ouch... I can see why he's so fascinated by you. You're sharp, witty, unimpressed with his wealth—and beautiful. A true rarity." He offered a mock bow, his eyes dancing with delight. "Nikos Aetos. At your service. We were never formally introduced."

Her fingers tightened slightly on the tray. "Can I offer you an hors d'oeuvre, Mr. Aetos?"

He looked down at the tray, then back at her, the glint in his eyes sharpening. "Not tonight. I'm here to play interference—and stop you from escaping again."

She blinked in surprise. "Excuse me?"

He leaned in conspiratorially. "I was sent to stall you—for Theo."

Her mouth fell open, words colliding uselessly on her tongue.

He chuckled. "You're fast for someone hauling crab cakes."

Rose took a step back, glancing over her shoulder when she bumped into someone—and groaned.

Theo was standing right behind her.

His dark gaze locked on her, hunger and frustration simmering just beneath the surface.

"You sold me out," she accused Nikos, glaring back at him.

He shrugged, unapologetic. "You aren't easy to catch—and friends need to stick together."

"Well, you might want to consider finding better friends."

"Not a very subtle one, Theo," Nikos chuckled, sipping his drink with a wink. "I like her."

"I'm going to dump this entire tray on your fancy Italian shoes. Let's see how you like me after you walk in crabmeat and cream cheese."

"It would be worth it," Nikos laughed.

"Toad," Rose muttered.

"Are you two finished, Nikos? If so, thank you, I'll take it from here."

Nikos lifted his glass in salute. "Break a leg." Then he sauntered off, leaving her alone with the man who haunted her sleep.

Rose's breath caught, and she turned slowly to face Theo. Being this close to him was like standing near a flame—thrilling and terrifying.

She opened her mouth—nothing came out.

"Rose." His voice was low—soft, reverent... dangerous.

She swallowed.

"You can't keep avoiding me."

"I'm working," she replied stiffly.

He looked down at the tray, then gently took it from her hands and set it on a nearby table.

"That's better," he said.

Her hands felt empty, leaving her feeling awkward and unsure. Her pulse pounded in her throat as she stared up at him.

"This isn't a fairy tale," she whispered.

His eyes gleamed. "Then why does it feel like one?"

It felt like one to him. All he wanted to do was sweep her into his arms and walk out of the damn theatre.

Just... scoop her up, carry her down the marbled steps like the Beast escaping into his castle with his Beauty, and shut the rest of the world out behind them.

She was right—this wasn't a fairytale.

But damn if he didn't feel like the monster in one. And she... she was the one thing tethering him to something good. Something unique.

Instead, Theo inhaled deeply, steadying himself. His fingers flexed at his sides. Patience—once a virtue he prided himself on—was proving far more elusive when Rose was in the same room. She made it hard to think. Hard to breathe.

"I'd like to see you again," he said softly.

She tilted her head, her dark lashes briefly brushing her cheeks before she studied him with those soul-deep eyes. "Why?"

One word—simple, innocent. But it sucker-punched him.

Why?

No one had ever asked him that before. Ever. They'd smiled, flirted, angled for more, but never once questioned why he wanted to see them.

His mouth opened—then closed again.

Rose arched a delicate eyebrow. "What's the matter? Cat got your tongue? It wasn't a very difficult question, you know."

A low chuckle slipped from her lips, warm and amused. But it wasn't cruel. It was… delighted.

And that hit even harder.

He let out a quiet groan and rubbed the back of his neck. "God, this is bruising my ego. Even as a teenager, I didn't have to work this hard."

"Interesting—and disappointing if women fall that easily," she mused, a frown creasing her brow. "Or, perhaps you simply have a weakness for women who like strong, wealthy, handsome men that aren't picky. Honestly, there is so much to contemplate in that single admittance that it may take me a lifetime to analyze it," she murmured, her voice a low hum, her smile barely there, but there was a wicked glimmer of amusement in them that made her eyes sparkle.

His cheeks flushed. His cheeks! He could feel the warmth rising from under his collar. He couldn't remember the last time that had happened—or if it ever had.

"You're enjoying this far too much," he accused, not quite able to hide the grin tugging at the corner of his mouth.

She shrugged one delicate shoulder. "Maybe a little." She paused. "So... are you asking me out? Like—on a date?"

He nodded, clearing his throat. "Yes. I want to see you again. Outside of all... this." He gestured to the swirl of people and champagne. "You and me. Just us."

She hesitated, as if weighing the idea of whether they should be alone together.

He held himself still while she studied him again. For the first time in a long, long time, he felt... seen. Not as a billionaire. Not as Theo Kallistratos, the name on boardroom doors, glossy magazine covers, or tabloid pages. Just a man, standing in front of a woman, hoping she'd say yes.

Rose's lips quirked, slow and deliberate. "One date."

Relief crashed through him like a wave.

"I want more than—" he started.

She shot him a pointed look and shook her head.

"One date—then we'll see if there will be another," she added.

"I'll take it," he said, exhaling a breath he hadn't realized he was holding. "Tomorrow morning—unless you want to—"

She released a snort of laughter and shook her head again. He grinned at her swift, silent glare of admonishment.

It was worth trying.

"Tomorrow night," she corrected, already stepping back. "I have a lot of work to do in the morning."

He opened his mouth to ask what kind of work—but before he could, Mimi appeared in a cloud of designer perfume and sequins.

"Oh, Theo! There you are! Did you get a chance to meet my husband?" she beamed, tugging his arm with surprising strength for a woman pushing sixty.

He glanced back—just in time to see Rose disappearing into the crowd again, her tray back in hand, her ponytail swinging with each step.

Gone—like Cinderella at the stroke of midnight.

Only this time, she hadn't left a glass slipper. She'd given a promise. One date.

As Mimi launched into a spirited monologue about her original casting of a character from her first production, Theo's mind barely registered a word.

Because an idea had formed.

Something bold. Reckless, maybe. But that didn't matter.

He wanted her.

Not just for a night. Not just for the chase.

All in.

If Rose thought one kiss—or one date—would satisfy him, she didn't know how determined the Beast could be.

He was going to win her heart—

And he wasn't above using a bit of his money, power, and ruthlessness to get it.

He listened to Mimi Devan twaddle on before he turned to her. "Mrs. Devan—Mimi—I would like a tour of the theatre. I'm considering making a rather substantial donation."

"Really? I—That would be lovely," Mimi stammered, her eyes wide with excitement.

"Perhaps tomorrow morning?" he asked.

"Tomorrow morning—of course. Tomorrow would be absolutely doable," Mimi preened, smiling brightly back at him.

"Wonderful. Will Rose be available as well?"

Mimi frowned, glancing around the room before her eyes landed on

Rose, smiling and offering refreshments. His gaze had been locked on Rose the entire time.

"I—well, I suppose so. She does maintenance for the theatre," Mimi replied.

"Good. Then she will know everything there is to know about it," he said, pleased. "I didn't catch Rose's last name."

"It's Smythe—Rose Smythe," Mimi's husband answered.

"Smith?" His eyes widened with surprise.

"Yes. No relation to Bob and Beverly, Joan and Clint, or Harold and Sue," Claude Devan answered with amusement, nodding at a half-dozen other patrons in the crowd.

Theo grimaced, acknowledging how common the name was. Still, it was enough to remind him that he still had his promise to locate Lorenzo's granddaughter hanging over his head. Maybe he should turn the search over to Nikos and his brother.

"Darling, the mayor is about to leave, and I think it would be nice if you said your goodbyes, as he is having a meeting about the Arts funding next week," Claude murmured.

"Oh, yes. Tomorrow, Mr. Kallistratos. Say, ten—ten-thirty?" Mimi asked, already turning as her husband cupped her elbow.

"I'll see you at ten."

He lifted the glass of whiskey to his lips, his eyes following Rose as she exchanged trays with another server, laughing at whatever the man said, before she turned away. Their eyes met again across the room.

Fire burned through him when he noticed the hint of pink in her face and the way she shielded the look in her eyes by lowering her eyelashes. She wasn't flirting with him—she was trying to build a wall.

"You're about to set the fire alarms off," Nikos commented, coming to stand next to him.

"Shut up."

Nikos snickered and sipped his drink. "I like her."

Jealousy reared its ugly head and exploded through him like a fuse to a powder keg. He turned a sharp gaze to his friend. Nikos shook his head in amusement.

"I like her *for you*. If any woman can keep you from stepping all over her, I think that one can," Nikos clarified.

Theo sighed, studying his friend's expression. "Why do I feel there is a 'but' in your observation," he said.

"But… she is also very different from the women you normally date," Nikos added.

Theo heard the hint of caution and concern—not for him, but for Rose —in his friend's voice. He knew Rose wasn't like the other women he dated. She was nothing like his former mistresses, all of whom knew the rules.

Hell, when it came to rules, he was the one who wasn't sure he knew them now. He placed his empty glass on the tray of a passing server, his eyes narrowing moodily as he continued to watch Rose.

"What are you planning? Or should I ask?" Nikos muttered, finishing his drink and depositing his glass as well.

"Closing the gates. This time, she won't escape me," he confessed, shoving his hands into his pockets.

A flicker of unease tugged at him—but he pushed it aside. This wasn't control. It was… time. And he would buy all the time he needed.

Nikos shot him a wary glance. "Are you sure that is a good idea with this one? Something tells me she won't like it if she finds out."

"She won't, but who says she needs to find out? I need to turn the search for Lorenzo's granddaughter over to you," he said.

"Well, that sounds like fun," Nikos muttered. "It looks like things are wrapping up here. Do you want to go to the club for a while?"

"No, you go. I think I'll stick around for a little longer," he murmured.

"I'll console all the lovely ladies, offering a comforting shoulder as they mourn their loss."

Theo shook his head as Nikos departed, his laughter fading along with the chatter of the other guests. He was already locked onto where Rose was collecting discarded glasses and plates.

# Seven

The after-party had dwindled to an echo. Only the shuffle of clean-up remained—discarded flutes, scattered napkins, and glitter that would outlive them all.

Rose froze mid-wipe. Theo Kallistratos—billionaire, enigma, temptation in black—was stacking dishes. Helping.

She chuckled under her breath, shaking her head and wondering if exhaustion was playing tricks on her. But no, he was very much real and helping clean up.

A member of the catering team noticed him too. The man's eyes widened with a touch of awe.

"We've got it from here, sir," the man said, his voice tinged with bemusement.

Theo nodded and stepped aside, handing off the full tray without fanfare.

Rose smiled faintly, her heart thudding too fast. "You and your crew did a wonderful job," she told the man. He grinned, gave a half-bow, and disappeared into the kitchen.

She discreetly wiped her palms on her slacks and turned to Theo.

He turned too—toward her.

Neither of them spoke. Another server passed between them, breaking the moment as she collected the last of the glasses from a table. Rose jerked her head toward the side hallway and motioned for him to follow.

For a moment, she wasn't sure where to go. She just… needed to move, to escape the stillness.

They walked in silence, a comfortable quiet, yet the air shimmered with an unspoken connection—like a shared secret.

When he reached down and gently laced his fingers through hers, she felt a jolt of excitement and her heart skipped. She led him up a narrow staircase hidden behind a plush velvet curtain, each step a quiet footfall on the threadbare carpet.

"Careful," she murmured. "These stairs are older than half the city."

They emerged onto the upper balcony. The lights were dimmed except for the soft golden illumination from the sconces on the wall. The hush of the theatre wrapped around them, thick and velvet-soft.

Theo took it all in—rows of burgundy seats cascading down to the stage below, the grand chandelier overhead, and the walls adorned with sepia-toned photographs in gilded frames.

"This place was built in 1908," Rose said softly, reverently. "By a Hungarian architect named István Solokov. He designed it for his wife, a famous soprano who performed across Europe. When she passed, he swore he'd never set foot inside again. Performers say her voice still lingers in the acoustics."

She looked around, trying to see the theatre through his eyes. Her gaze swept over the curve of the balcony, the intricate molding, and the portraits of long-forgotten stars.

"Some of the greats performed here," she continued. "Tallulah Bankhead. Paul Robeson. Even Charlie Chaplin, once, when his train was delayed—he borrowed a violin and played by candlelight."

Her voice warmed as she spoke. A light flush of self-awareness flashed through her when she noticed that Theo watched her more than the theatre.

"You sound like you really know the history of this building," he commented.

She nodded, tucking a strand of loose hair behind her ear. "My grandparents took over the maintenance and design when my grandmother was expecting my dad. My grandfather built most of the set pieces you saw tonight. I helped. The candelabra you passed earlier? That was ours."

Theo turned back toward the walls, taking in the legacy. "The stage pieces were beautiful."

"My grandfather knew how to create true magic," she whispered. "Would you like to know a secret?"

His eyes sharpened with interest, and he nodded.

She wiggled her nose at him and smiled. "Even though I know how everything works, even when I've seen a backdrop collapse during intermission or scrambled to find a missing costume, the magic still hits me. That moment when the lights dim, the music swells, and you forget everything else—it's magical. I love it."

"Did you ever want to be on stage?"

She laughed, the sound light and carefree. "No. My grandparents and parents were the performers in the family. I love being behind the curtain. Helping tell the story… not being the character."

"So… what else do you do? Besides being a jack-of-all-trades?"

She hesitated and released another self-conscious laugh. "I just finished my Bachelor's degree in accounting and economics. Glamorous, right?"

He smiled, his lips curving in quiet surprise. "Smart and creative. There's nothing wrong with that."

"That's what my Pop said," she confessed.

They continued walking, climbing higher and higher, until they stood on the catwalk above the stage. Below them, the ballroom set glowed under the ambient light. Rose realized that she had guided Theo to the spot where their eyes had met earlier this evening. From here, the entire lower theatre spread before them.

She gestured toward the area to the left below them.

"That staircase? We rebuilt it four times. There was a leak, and the directors didn't want to spend the money to have the roof fixed. They did—after water damage caused a lot more damage. Pop kept telling them. The chandelier is real crystal; my grandfather was terrified when the company reinstalling it after it was taken down for a cleaning nearly dropped it."

He looked at her with a quiet intensity. "You said your grandparents raised you?"

Her smile dimmed. "Yeah. My parents were in a car accident. My mom died instantly. My dad lived… but he was in a coma and never woke. He passed away when I was five. It nearly broke my grandparents."

Theo's eyes softened, but she shook her head gently before she glanced at her watch.

"It's late. I need to check the doors and make sure everything is locked up."

He nodded. Together they descended the stairs, their footsteps echoing softly through the theatre's empty halls.

"I love that I'm walking the same place that so many others have before me. Sometimes I like to imagine I can see and hear them— dressed in their period clothing, laughing about the performance they just saw," she sighed, feeling a little self-conscious about sharing such an intimate feeling with him.

She checked each door—methodically, automatically. He didn't offer to help, just stayed beside her. Silent. Present.

When they reached the last door, she turned awkwardly, brushing her palms down her slacks again.

"So… I guess I'll see you tomorrow night?" she asked, glancing up at him. "What time? And where?"

"Is seven too early?" he asked.

"No, that's perfect. I rarely stay out late," she said with a small shrug.

"I'd like to escort you home," he said, his brow pulling together.

She laughed. "You already have." She turned and waved her hand behind them.

He looked at her with a confused frown. "What do you mean?"

"I live here. In the basement. Perks of handling maintenance. Awesome responsibility and itty-bitty living accommodations."

Theo stared at her, then let out a soft, stunned breath of laughter. Of course she did. Rose Smythe belonged to the theatre, body and soul.

She pulled open the main door, the cool night air brushing her cheeks. "Will you be okay getting home?"

He didn't answer, just lifted a hand.

A sleek black car slid to a stop at the curb.

"Ah, right," she murmured.

He glanced back and chuckled. "Perks of being a billionaire."

She stepped outside to walk him to the car, but he turned back—swift and deliberate.

He brushed his lips across hers. Feather-light—and it stole her breath.

His voice was low, husky, and wrecked. "That kiss doesn't count."

She stared up at him, dazed.

"I'll see you tomorrow. Lock the door behind me," he added, retreating toward the car.

She nodded, barely breathing. "Goodnight, Theo."

The car door shut, and he was gone.

She closed the door, turned the bolt—and just stood there. The lobby was empty, still, and glowing with a soft amber hush.

She lifted her fingers to her lips.

Grinning like a fool, she spun in a circle, laughing breathlessly, and danced through the lobby, down the narrow stairs, and into the small, quiet world she called home.

She felt like a girl in a fairytale who'd just danced with the Prince—and wasn't ready for midnight.

The faint gleam of Manhattan's dawn seeped through the shades, casting long lines across the sharp geometry of his minimalist bedroom. Concrete, steel, and glass—cold and efficient, like the man who built an empire inside it.

Theo woke with a jolt. His breath caught in his chest, as if he'd been yanked from a dream he wasn't ready to leave.

Or maybe it was the dream that refused to release him.

He lay still for a moment, his breath even, his heart steady—but his mind was already racing.

Rose.

His dreams had centered on her. The gentle, sensual sound of her laugh. Her stubbornness. Her wicked sense of humor.

A soft grunt—half groan, half dry laughter—slipped from him when he thought of the kiss that didn't count.

*How could such an innocent gesture create so much chaos inside me?*

He grimaced at the covers—this wasn't routine morning arousal but the echo of his dream of her.

Her smile lingered behind his eyelids, teasing him with delicate lips and dark, sapphire eyes that were unreadable. The phantom feel of her kiss—light as a whisper—still burned like embers on his skin.

He blinked at the ceiling, then rolled to sit up.

The clock on his nightstand flashed half-past six.

He'd gone to bed a little after three, his mind too wired to sleep. And yet here he was—wide awake.

His body only ever demanded three or four hours—enough to recharge, never enough to distract him from what needed doing.

And this morning, there was plenty.

By seven, he was showered, shaved, and dressed in a crisp, tailored navy suit with no tie. Impeccable. Sharp enough to cut glass. The way he always appeared when he wanted something—and fully intended to get it.

He strolled into the kitchen, the scent of fresh-brewed coffee curling in the air. As he entered, Mrs. Hughes, his long-time housekeeper, nearly dropped the set of silverware she'd been arranging.

"Mr. Kallistratos!" she gasped. "I was just about to bring your coffee in."

Theo chuckled as he grabbed a mug and poured himself coffee. "No need. I wanted to let you know there will be two for breakfast. Nikos and I have a meeting."

Mrs. Hughes blinked, her gray curls bobbing slightly. "Shall I bring your breakfast to your office?"

"The dining room is fine," he replied with a grin.

"I'll add some nice pastries from the corner shop to the menu. Mr. Aetos loves those," she said with a pleased smile.

He chuckled, the sound echoing slightly, as he exited the bright, modern kitchen. He was heading to the dining room when a brief, sharp knock and the distinct click of the penthouse door announced Nikos's expected early arrival.

He paused, scrutinizing Nikos's appearance. "Did you even go to bed last night, or did you just grab a shower?"

"I could ask you the same thing. I'm assuming since you've already texted me this morning, you're up and dressed, *and* you're in the penthouse instead of a hotel room that you weren't able to sweet-talk your beautiful Rose into spending the night with you," Nikos commented, not answering his question.

Theo shot Nikos a warning look but held back the sharp reply as Mrs. Hughes appeared. He motioned to Nikos to have a seat.

"When are you going to quit serving this horrid man and come work for me?" Nikos teased.

"When cows learn to fly," Mrs. Hughes retorted.

Nikos laughed and placed his hand over his heart. "I'm wounded."

"That's why I had these delivered, to soften the blow," Mrs. Hughes chuckled, lifting a silver lid to reveal the platter of pastries.

"I'm in love. Tell Mr. Hughes he is a very lucky man," Nikos said with a delighted groan as he reached for an apricot-filled Danish.

"Oh, he knows," Mrs. Hughes laughed before she left them alone.

"Are you finished trying to steal my housekeeper away?" Theo asked drily.

"Not even close," Nikos replied. He lifted his fork and waved it at Theo. "So, your early morning text was a little vague—*Breakfast, ASAP.* There wasn't much to go on there."

Theo opened his laptop. The report he had requested from his PA in Greece was waiting for him. He opened the file, scanning it.

Within seconds, he was deep in a rabbit hole of old records, restoration permits, tax documents, and historic preservation grants.

The Gerster Theatre was a marvel—underfunded, underappreciated, but rich with legacy. With every photo he pulled up, every news article he scanned, his fascination deepened.

"It's an old structure—original design from 1908. Hungarian architect. Amazing craftsmanship," he said absently.

Nikos lifted an eyebrow. "This is about Rose, isn't it?"

"She lives there. Works there. It's her entire world." Theo scrolled down.

"That's… fascinating. What does this have to do with me being here at the crack of dawn?" Nikos asked dryly, stabbing a piece of bacon with his fork.

Theo shot him a look, unimpressed.

"Her grandfather, Alfred Smythe, immigrated from Scotland. Her grandmother, Iris, was Irish. They were performers before they transitioned to design and set building. That theatre—it's a legacy project."

Theo finally closed his laptop, rolled his shoulders and focused on his breakfast.

"Fascinating—and still doesn't answer my question," Nikos said, nodding at him with a curious expression. "What happened after I left last night? Did she slap you or kiss you?"

"Neither. She did agree to go out with me tonight."

"I guess that's progress—though, I have to say, this is a bit—unusual— for you," Nikos murmured.

Theo scowled. "I'm going to surprise her this morning."

Nikos set his fork down slowly. "Theo. What are you up to?"

"I have a meeting with Mimi Devan. The theatre director."

Nikos's eyes narrowed. "Why?"

"I'm going to make a sizable donation."

"In exchange for what?"

Theo sipped his coffee. He didn't answer right away. Instead, he leaned back in his chair, his gaze steady.

"I plan to woo Rose," he said simply.

"That I can understand. She is the type of woman who needs wooing. It's the undertone that I don't like." Nikos stared at him before he released a sigh and flatly asked, "In exchange for what? You don't do anything without a purpose."

Theo exhaled. "Time. I want Rose, and I can't be with her if she is busy elsewhere."

Nikos cursed softly in Greek and shook his head.

"Why do I get the sinking feeling I'm not going to like what you mean by that?"

He shrugged. When he saw a problem, he solved it. In this case, he wanted Rose. The problem was she was busy—and so was he. His need to travel around the world would cause issues. The simplest solution was to free Rose from her schedule—and offer her the world in return.

"I'm due in London, then Paris, Athens, and Rome. I need her free to come with me."

"And you don't see a problem with the fact that she might not want to go? What if she finds out you were behind her suddenly free schedule?"

Theo shrugged. "She won't find out. And if she does—she'll see it was for us."

"Jesus, Theo. Try thinking with the head above your shoulders," Nikos scowled.

Theo's jaw flexed. "I know what I'm doing."

"You don't think this is a little arrogant? Even for you? You think she'll be flattered? That you've traded money for time with her? What if she sees it as control? Manipulation?"

He didn't flinch—outwardly. "It's not manipulation. It's speeding up the inevitable."

"You're making a lot of assumptions. I believe the term I've heard before is 'Putting the cart before the horse'. It might be better if you—I don't know—maybe ask her what she wants," Nikos muttered. He stopped, released a low chuckle, and blew out a breath. "Hell. What am I talking about? I wouldn't know what to do if I had a woman playing hard to get. It seems like too much work. Give me a nice, amiable woman who only wants one thing—as long as it isn't marriage —and I'm happy. Who knows, maybe everything will work out fine. It did for Alexandros. All I've got to say is good luck."

"I need to ask a favor," he said, breathing a sigh of relief as he changed the topic.

"Of course, provided it doesn't include abducting that beautiful young woman you're so enamored with."

"I'd like you to review the leads I have so far on Lorenzo's granddaughter. There isn't much. I feel like I'm missing something," he confessed.

"You could've handed this off to one of our teams," Nikos pointed out.

"I would, but I promised Lorenzo I would keep this quiet. I don't think he told Sophia, Lucinda, or Raff about the photo."

Nikos nodded. "I can understand that. It would be terrible to say Livia had a child, only to discover there wasn't one."

"My thoughts exactly. I've added all my notes, including the interview with the old woman who lived next door to them into the file," he said.

"Did she have any kids? If so, maybe one of them remembers more. I'll do some more research and get back to you. Do you know what you're going to do when you finally find her—if she exists that is?"

Theo shrugged and lifted an eyebrow. "What woman wouldn't be thrilled to find out she's the heir to a noble, obscenely wealthy Italian dynasty?"

Nikos threw back his head and laughed. "True. True."

# Eight

Morning cloaked the theatre in tranquility, curling around Rose like an old friend.

She paused by the controls in the auditorium, turning on the rows of lighting from above so she could see. Even the harsh lights couldn't dull the nostalgia. Nothing could.

Dust motes danced like tiny stars caught in the stream of light over the stage.

The world outside was just beginning to wake, but within these aging walls of magic and memory, Rose enjoyed the peace and quiet.

She moved along the rows like a ghost, tending each section with a loving hand. She hummed as she swept the rows, slowly working her way to the stage. This time of day had always belonged to her and her grandfather.

Long before the city woke, before the lights rose and the music swelled, these quiet hours were part of their sacred ritual. They'd hum fragments of the previous night's melodies, point out the scene that had gone sideways and the line that had unexpectedly soared. They'd sweep the stage together, trading stories and inside jokes, measuring time not in minutes but in moments.

Now, her grandfather's voice was only a memory.

She paused mid-sweep, staring out over the stage as the bristles stilled. The silence wasn't empty—it was filled with everything she missed.

Her gaze drifted to the grand piano at stage left.

It resembled the one in the Beast's castle—carved scrollwork, rose-gold trim—but beneath the glamour, it was a working instrument. A heavy, beloved thing that had been decorated repeatedly depending on the play.

Her grandfather had tuned it like an altar—devout, precise, and reverent.

Wordlessly, she set the broom aside and walked toward it. Her fingers hovered over the keys, hesitant, trembling slightly. She hadn't touched the ivory keys since her grandfather's death—and they felt colder now, heavier somehow.

She sat down slowly, her spine straight, posed like her grandmother had taught her.

She exhaled, her fingers caressing the smooth surface before she began to play.

At first, it was just single notes. Wandering tones that had no place to go.

A tentative smile curved her lips as the notes seeped into her soul, calling to her, awakening her love for music. Piece by piece, her fingers began to find the notes rising in her mind. The chords came—tentative, like the start of a thought. Then deeper, fuller, as an image rose to replace her uncertainty.

*Theo.*

She didn't try to stop the memory of him. She let it come—his voice in the dark, his smile when he looked at her like she was the only woman on earth.

Her fingers moved faster, coaxing life into the melody. Not written. Not remembered. Just... hers.

A song just for him.

A song of love and longing.

A world bloomed behind her closed eyes: she and Theo, barefoot in a candlelit ballroom that existed only in dreams. His hand pressed low against her back. Her laughter rose like champagne bubbles as he twirled her under gilded archways. The dark gleam in his eyes before he pulled her close again.

Her lips parted before she realized she was singing, the notes shaping into words she hadn't meant to release.

Her voice was husky, low, edged with a tremble that made it richer, more human.

She sang of what could never be spoken aloud.

Of wanting.

Of being seen.

Of kisses that didn't count but felt like a beginning.

Of the fear that what was growing between them might be real—

—and that it might vanish like all good things in her life had.

Her voice cracked. She faltered, as if the poetic words held an unspoken tragedy.

She thought of Theo pulling away after that kiss, of the way he'd stood so still before turning into the night.

She thought of what it would feel like when he didn't come back. When she watched him walk away for the last time.

The final chord held beneath her fingers, vibrating with loss and longing. And then it was gone. A breath. A whisper.

A memory already fading.

She bowed her head over the keys. Her hands slipped into her lap, trembling now.

That was the thing about the songs she created.

Her songs were ghosts—haunting for a moment, then gone, forgotten as soon as the echo died. They were just… snapshots that captured her emotions, a fragile thread of her life.

She inhaled slowly, blinking back the burning in her eyes.

She sighed and looked up. Her eyes widened with surprise, and she could feel her cheeks flush.

Theo was standing less than a dozen feet away from her, just beyond the shadows of the side stage.

Her gaze swept over him, unfiltered. A fierce longing to touch him—to taste him—rose like fire in her veins.

When their eyes locked, a deep, sensual awareness rose inside her in response to the look in his eyes.

He looked struck by lightning—stunned, every inch of him alive. His lips were parted, his eyes blazed with raw, unguarded desire.

Rose placed her hand over her thundering heart. Heat poured through her, settling low and throbbing in answer to his silent request.

She didn't remember rising.

Didn't remember closing the space between them.

She knew only that her hands reached for him first, her fingers curling in the lapel of his jacket, her chest rising with each shallow breath.

She felt his arms wrap around her, a warm and welcome haven. She breathed in his aftershave, a subtle, masculine fragrance that sent a shaft of need through her. She gave in to the ache, needing to touch him, to feel the warmth of his skin, to anchor herself in something real.

Her lips crashed into his, frantic, hungry. This time, the kiss counted.

His mouth was warm, insistent, less a question than an answer.

She kissed him with wild abandon. If there were rules, she was past caring. With her emotions on fire, she wanted to relish the exquisite sensations that sparked to life with his gentle touch.

One of his hands cupped her jaw, his thumb sweeping her cheek before he tangled it in her hair. His other hand swept lower, and he lifted her, pressing her against his body until they were aligned and she could feel his desire.

Their breaths tangled.

The stage disappeared beneath them.

Only the two of them remained, suspended in a world where a kiss was more than a kiss.

The moment Theo stepped into the lobby of The Gerster Theatre, he was met with warmth that had nothing to do with temperature. It also had nothing to do with the theatre itself.

No, the warmth came from knowing that Rose was here.

He smiled politely at the secretary who had opened the door. She stood quickly, flustered, clearly aware of who he was.

"Good morning, Mr. Kallistratos," she said, smoothing the front of her blouse. "You're early. Mrs. Devan hasn't arrived yet, but she texted just a few minutes ago. She should be here shortly."

"That's perfectly fine," he said smoothly. "I don't mind waiting."

He leaned against the counter just slightly, letting his presence fill the space—not imposing, but undeniable.

She blinked at him, her cheeks warming as she attempted a smile.

"Actually," he added, his tone thoughtful, "I wonder… Could Rose show me around while I wait?"

The secretary's brows lifted, then quickly furrowed. "I—I believe she's in the auditorium, doing her morning clean. I could go find her for you if you'd like—"

Theo raised a hand, that quiet, confident charm brushing through his voice like silk. "No need. I'll find my way."

Before she could protest, he offered a parting smile and moved down the hallway, his footsteps muffled against the thick carpet.

The grand foyer yawned open ahead of him, all gilded moldings and polished banisters. But his focus was beyond it—through the set of double doors that marked the heart of the building.

From behind them came a soft sound.

Music.

Piano—light, tentative, like a story being whispered instead of told.

He slowed, frowning slightly. Someone else was here.

His fingers brushed the brass doorknob, disappointment creeping in. But the moment he opened the door, that feeling shattered.

There she was.

Rose.

Alone at the piano, a broom forgotten and leaning against an ornate chair. Her head bowed slightly, the light from an overhead spotlight casting a halo over her hair.

She didn't see him.

And God help him, he couldn't move.

The notes shifted as he stood at the back of the darkened theatre. Random chords became something deliberate—gentle, aching, full of hope and heartbreak. Then, she began to sing.

Her voice wrapped around him like velvet. It was husky and pure, raw and reverent.

He felt like an intruder—but he couldn't look away. Every word, every trembling note, sounded like a confession pulled from her soul.

She sang of a man who didn't really see her.

Of wanting to be seen.

Of a kiss that didn't count—but had marked her just the same.

Theo swallowed hard, his fingers curling into fists at his sides.

She was singing about him.

And she had no idea he was there.

He moved slowly down the aisle, his eyes locked on her. Each step felt heavier than the last, burdened with a longing that had nowhere to go.

She was ethereal. Unreachable. Until she wasn't.

As he climbed the stairs to the stage, his chest ached with something unfamiliar. Reverence. Desire. Love. Not the love he knew from contracts and convenience. This was the love that made a man forget everything else—just to hear her sing for one more minute.

Her voice faltered on the last note. Her hands fell away from the keys.

And then she looked up.

Their eyes collided.

She looked stunned. A delicate blush rose to her cheeks, and her lips parted on a surprised breath, as if he'd been pulled from her imagination.

Theo didn't speak. Words would have ruined it.

He stepped closer.

His eyes devoured her as she rose gracefully from the piano bench. Her gaze never left his. Her hand lifted as if she needed to touch him.

The tension in his body dissolved when she wrapped her fingers in the lapel of his jacket.

He slid one hand along her cheek, cradling it for a moment as he tenderly ran his thumb across her lips before he wrapped it behind her nape and pulled her closer. His fingers tangled in her soft hair.

He leaned forward, savoring the moment—the weight of their connection, the sheer inevitability of them being together. She leaned into him, claiming his lips in a fiery kiss that unfurled the tension that had been building inside him.

Her lips parted for him, and he was lost.

The kiss was desperate, searching—like they had both been drifting for far too long and had finally come home.

He pressed her against him, needing to feel every inch of her. His hands slid down, wrapping around her waist, then lower, until he cupped the swell of her backside. He lifted her into him with a low groan, his arousal hard and aching against her belly.

She gasped softly into his mouth, her arms wrapping around his neck, holding him like he might vanish.

Their breaths tangled. The theatre faded.

There was no audience, no past, no future.

Only this stage. This kiss.

Her lips were soft and warm—like they were made for him.

He explored her mouth with aching need, making love to her with his lips and tongue. She met him stroke for stroke, breath for breath, clinging to him with the same intensity that burned through him. His need for her nearly gutted him in the best way.

His hand slid up her spine, memorizing the feel of her. She pressed closer, her chest rising and falling in fast, shallow breaths that matched his as they fought to get closer. His hand slipped under the hem of her sweatshirt, beneath the light t-shirt behind it, to her warm flesh.

He could have stayed like that forever.

But forever was fragile.

And reality was intruding.

Faint voices echoed in the distance—muffled at first, then clearer. Approaching. His desire fought with the need to protect Rose.

A reluctant groan escaped his lips as he ended the kiss. With his eyes closed, he leaned in, resting his forehead gently against hers. His chest heaved as he pulled in ragged breaths and tried to steady himself. He paused, savoring the moment before letting her go.

"We've got company," he murmured, his voice husky and thick. "Mimi's here."

He felt the shift in her body instantly—rigid awareness flooding her limbs like cold water. Her hands slowly dropped from around his neck. Her breath caught, and she turned her head slightly, not meeting his gaze.

She took a small step back.

His hands slid down her arms, lingering as long as he could before he let her go. Every cell in his body protested their separation.

Her face was flushed, her lips kiss-swollen and parted, her chest heaving as much as his. She lowered her eyelashes, refusing to look at him.

His heart thumped.

She was so beautiful.

So vulnerable.

*And I want her to be mine.*

He reached for her again, desperate to offer something—reassurance, comfort, anything—but the doors at the top of the auditorium groaned open, and Mimi's theatrical voice filled the vast space like a trumpet fanfare.

"Theo, *darling*! The mayor and his wife are still buzzing about seeing you last night, and now the rest of New York will be too!" she called, bustling inside with her secretary hurrying behind her, a folder clutched to her chest.

Rose bowed her head, lifted a shaky hand to brush her hair back, and took another step away from him. The moment folded in on itself, vanishing as quickly as it had bloomed.

Theo clenched his fists.

Her expression was closed off now. Composed. But her movements gave her away—the slight tremble in her fingers as she retrieved the broom from where it rested against a chair, the way she didn't look at him as she turned away, her body humming with restraint.

He took a step forward.

"Rose—"

She shook her head, just once. Soft. Final.

It wasn't rejection.

It was a silent plea.

*Let this moment go—for now.*

He wavered as she walked off toward the side of the stage, disappearing behind the velvet curtain and into the shadows where she could breathe again.

Theo exhaled slowly, forcing his pulse to even out. A low growl of frustration rumbled in his chest.

She was slipping behind the curtain again—figuratively and literally.

And he wasn't about to let that happen.

Not again.

*Not ever,* he thought as the primitive urge to announce to the world that Rose was his woman swept through him.

He turned with frustration toward the sound of footsteps echoing across the wooden floor.

Mimi ascended the steps like a queen in stilettos, ready to conquer.

"My word," she beamed, sweeping her arms out like she was taking a bow. "You're even more handsome in the morning light. How is that fair?"

Theo forced a polite smile. "Mrs. Devan. Thank you for seeing me on such short notice."

Mimi's secretary handed off the folder and scurried out of the theatre at her boss's not-so-subtle wave. Mimi turned her full attention on him now, her eyes bright with curiosity, barely restrained excitement, and more than a little bit of avarice.

He walked in silence as Mimi began her sales pitch. Her voice fluttered with praise about his reputation for supporting the arts, the legacy of the theatre, and how thrilled she was by his interest.

Theo nodded, murmuring appropriate responses, but his mind wasn't on her.

It was on the woman who had disappeared earlier backstage.

The one who'd kissed him with wild abandon. He turned as he and Mimi returned to the stage a half-hour later. He could feel Rose's eyes on him.

Looking up, he scanned the upper levels of the theatre. She was his Christine Daaé from *Le Fantôme de l'Opéra*—only she was held captive by her memories here in the theatre.

*That ends today.*

The decision clicked into place, ruthless in its logic. A pang of doubt whispered at the edge of his conscience—but he silenced it. He would not lose her.

There would be no more disappearing into the shadows. He would offer Mimi the donation—but in return, he would ask her to let Rose go. Not immediately. He needed time. He needed Rose to trust him… to want to come with him.

But the end goal was now set in stone.

He wasn't just going to woo her. He would rewrite her world—whatever it took.

# Nine

Rose stood before the dressing room mirror beneath the stage, smoothing her palms over the pale blue cocktail gown. The fabric shimmered under the old vanity lights, catching silver flecks hidden in the tulle. Her heart was pounding—and it had nothing to do with the snug bodice or the unfamiliar feel of satin against her thighs.

The dress had been designed by her grandmother for a lavish production of *West Side Story,* and it still carried the flash of curtain calls and spotlight dreams. As Rose had slipped into it, she couldn't help but think of Cinderella or Belle getting ready for their date with a prince. She twirled, her eyes lighting with delight as the filmy material swirled elegantly around her calves. She wasn't sure she ever wanted to take it off.

Behind her, Kerry let out a low whistle, stepping back to take in the full effect.

"Well, if the billionaire doesn't fall flat on his face when he sees you, I'll personally push him down the stairs," she declared, planting her hands on her hips.

Rose laughed, thin and breathless. "It's not that serious."

Kerry raised an eyebrow. "You're in a dress, glowing like a spotlight, and you've been smiling like it's opening night ever since you told me about the kiss you two shared on the stage this morning. I'd say it's serious enough."

Rose turned in a slow circle, the gown flaring around her like a blooming flower. For a moment, she let herself drift into the fantasy. Candlelight, music, Theo's hand reaching for hers beneath a starlit sky. Her throat tightened. She pressed one hand to her stomach.

"Nerves?" Kerry asked knowingly.

"Terrified. This is my first proper date—the ones with you don't count," Rose admitted with a small smile. "Theo and I haven't talked since... you know."

"Since you kissed the man like the last act of a Broadway love story?" Kerry teased, nudging her shoulder.

Rose laughed again, but her gaze dropped. "I don't know what this is. Maybe it's nothing, but he makes me—"

Her cheeks flared with color again.

"Maybe it's everything you've dreamed of. You deserve to be happy, Rose. Don't be afraid to reach for it." Kerry adjusted the delicate neckline of the dress before stepping back again. "Also, just putting it out there... If Theo bails, my brother Robby is in town."

Rose frowned. "Wait—Robby? The one who builds furniture and looks like he wrestles bears for fun?"

Kerry grinned. "The very one. He's here making a delivery for a big-name designer. Hates driving a box truck through the city but loves New Yorkers with money. And," she added with a wink, "he said if things don't work out with your billionaire, he wouldn't mind meeting the mystery girl who has kept his sister out of trouble."

Rose rolled her eyes, but her smile bloomed. "That's flattering. And slightly terrifying."

"Just options, girl," Kerry said with a shrug. "A wise woman never keeps all her tiaras in one trunk."

They both dissolved into helpless laughter. It felt good—effortless and light. For the first time since her grandfather's death, Rose felt lighter, younger, freer, and daring, as if a weight had lifted from her shoulders.

When Kerry checked the time, she grimaced. "Crap. I've gotta go. Robby's taking me out for pizza before he heads back tomorrow. He wants real New York pizza," she said in an exaggerated New York accent.

She reached for her coat, then paused, catching Rose in a sudden, fierce hug.

"You look beautiful—like, fairytale beautiful. Don't let that billionaire hurt you, or I swear, I'll hunt him down with my brother's lathe."

Rose hugged her back tightly, her eyes stinging. "I'll be okay. I promise. It's just… a night. A one-off."

Kerry hesitated, her eyebrows pulling together like she wanted to say more—but then she just pressed a kiss to Rose's cheek and whispered, "I want every detail tomorrow. Even the scandalous ones."

Rose smiled faintly. "Sure. Every detail."

Even though they both knew… she probably wouldn't.

Kerry left in a flurry of laughter and promises, her boots clicking up the hallway.

Twenty minutes later, Rose stepped out the side door into the service alley, her heart beating like a timpani beneath her ribs. She rounded the corner to the front, climbing the curved steps to stand beneath the covered entrance.

The theatre loomed behind her, a familiar cocoon. But tonight, she felt like a stranger to herself—like someone new had slipped into her skin and borrowed her name.

She was adjusting the silver shawl that went with her dress when a sleek black SUV pulled up to the curb. The back door opened, and Theo emerged in a tailored charcoal suit—cut to steal a woman's breath.

Rose gulped, licked her lips, and hoped she wouldn't embarrass herself by drooling.

Theo paused on the first step, his eyes devouring her with a silent hunger that caused an unfamiliar heat to pool between her legs and spread outward.

For a beat, neither of them moved.

A slow, devastating smile curved across his lips. His eyes darkened, roving over her with a hunger that made her pulse skitter.

"You…" he said, his voice rough. "You're—stunning."

Color rushed to her cheeks, but she managed a smile. "I, uh, raided the costume storage. I wasn't sure jeans and a sweatshirt would be considered date-worthy attire."

He didn't answer. Instead, he moved up the steps, each stride a promise.

He took her hand in his. "Whatever you wear is perfect. Wearing nothing would be even better," he murmured—and then, without waiting, he pulled her into his arms and kissed her.

It wasn't tentative. It wasn't polite. It was a claim.

His lips captured hers with a hunger that stole her breath, one hand braced at her lower back, the other tangling in her dark, shoulder-length curls. Her lips parted when he deepened the kiss.

She clutched at his jacket, dizzy with sensation. There was nothing gentle about this kiss. Hell, there had been nothing gentle about any of their kisses. Even the one he had brushed across her lips had felt wild and untamed.

That was fine with her. She didn't want gentle. She wanted this. Him.

When he finally pulled back, his warm breath caressed her lips. His eyes held hers, unreadable and intense.

"Now I'm ready," he said, his voice low, nearly reverent.

He led her down the steps and into the car like she was royalty, his hand never leaving hers. She glanced at him as he gave the driver an address she didn't recognize.

He turned to her, his expression unreadable but soft at the edges.

"Trust me?" he asked.

She hesitated, then nodded. "Yes."

He hadn't planned this—at least, not the way it was unfolding. He hadn't planned the impulsive kiss on the steps or the rush of desire that nearly undid him in full view of the street.

Rose was breathtaking in the shimmering blue cocktail dress that clung to her like it had been made for her alone. His pulse was still racing, his mind at war with his body—one demanding restraint, the other wanting nothing more than to claim her now.

Her kiss that morning had set his world on fire and left it smoldering all day. He'd gone through meetings, calls with his father and brother, and couldn't recall a word of them. All he could think about was the way she had looked at him... the way she had kissed him like he was everything to her.

Now, sitting beside her in the back of the SUV, his hand resting lightly over hers, he could feel that storm rising again. He hadn't let go of her since she'd slid into the seat. It had taken every ounce of willpower not to pull her onto his lap and taste her again.

Instead, he'd given the driver an address where there would be no cameras and no interruptions.

His penthouse.

She turned to him, her brow knitting slightly. "Where are we going?"

Some of the earlier sparkle in her voice was gone, replaced by something quieter, more vulnerable.

He noticed the faint tremor in her fingers. His chest tightened. A wave of protectiveness washed over him.

"Somewhere we can talk," he said gently. "Without being overheard. Or distracted."

Her eyes lifted to his. She didn't pull away when he brought her hand to his lips and brushed a kiss across her knuckles.

He breathed a relieved sigh when the SUV pulled into the underground parking garage. He exited, holding his hand out to help Rose. They entered the garage-level elevator.

He released her hand and flashed his watch across the keypad interface.

The elevator ride to the penthouse was done in silence. He flexed his fingers, anticipation thrumming inside him. He didn't touch her—he couldn't—but he felt her presence like heat against his skin: the faint scent of her hair, the subtle rise and fall of her breath, the awareness coiled in the air between them like static before a storm.

When the doors slid open to reveal the skyline, she released a soft gasp. The Manhattan lights stretched endlessly in every direction, glittering like a thousand tiny stars.

The penthouse was sleek and masculine—steel, charcoal, glass—but softened by art and warm lighting. A castle built by a man who could have anything money could buy.

"My chef has prepared dinner," he told her, gesturing toward the table set for two near the terrace doors. "We can eat inside, or outside if it's not too cold."

"You have a personal chef?" she asked with a faint smile, her gaze roaming the room.

"Yes," he said, but her attention wasn't on the table anymore—it was on him.

He was about to offer to take her wrap when she moved. Her hands slid over his chest, up to his shoulders, before looping behind his neck. Her lips were on his in the next breath—hot, urgent, unguarded.

"Rose…" he murmured into her mouth. "Oh, my sweet Rose."

Desire roared through him, drowning every rational thought. He kissed her back, deepening the kiss until his head spun.

"What about—" he tried, breathless, "—dinner?"

"Later," she whispered against his lips.

Her fingers tugged at his jacket until it slid from his shoulders and fell to the floor. He groaned, reaching for the soft shawl around her. It slipped away like mist, revealing the curve of her shoulders and the way the dress hugged her every line.

"Is anyone else here?" she asked, her voice husky.

He shook his head. "No. Just us."

"Good."

She kicked off her heels, barefoot in his penthouse—like she'd always belonged there.

*God, she's killing me.*

Her kiss slowed, becoming exploratory, her fingertips tracing the bare skin of his chest where she'd already undone most of the buttons of his shirt. She was touching him as if she wanted to memorize him.

He let her, his hands moving over her hips, then lower to the small of her back, anchoring her against him. She arched into him, her body molding to his until every inch of him ached.

"Is it… always like this?" she asked softly.

The question cut through the haze. He stilled, drawing back enough to meet her eyes.

"What do you mean?"

Her cheeks flushed, but she didn't look away. "I mean… I've never…"

Understanding hit hard. "You've never been with anyone?"

She leaned in and kissed him, her lips brushing his as she murmured, "If I had, I wouldn't be asking."

The words lit something deep inside him—not just desire, but an overwhelming need to honor the trust she was giving him.

He groaned and kissed her again, fiercer this time, then swept her into his arms. She gasped and clung to him, her cheek against his shoulder.

"I've got you," he murmured.

"I know," she whispered.

He carried her down the hall to his bedroom, the city lights spilling across the floor-to-ceiling windows. The soft amber glow of the recessed lights bathed her in gold.

At the edge of the bed, he lowered her to stand on her feet slowly, keeping his forehead against hers. "You can stop me anytime. Just say the word.

Her fingers traced the line of his jaw down to his chest. "I don't want you to stop."

His breath left him in a shudder. He kissed her again—slower, deeper, full of wonder—before sliding the zipper of her dress down in a single smooth motion. The gown loosened and slipped away, pooling at her feet.

She stood before him in lace and bare feet, vulnerable and breathtaking.

"Yes," he said when she gave a nervous smile, "I'm staring."

Her laugh trembled into a gasp when he unclasped her bra. He took his time, his lips mapping her skin, his hands steady as he guided her backward onto the bed

When she arched into him, he knew he'd remember this moment for the rest of his life—not just for the heat, but for the way she looked at him... like he was already hers.

A slow, shy smile curved her lips.

When she didn't pull away, he bent to kiss her again. He started at her shoulders, moved to her neck, then to the soft curve of her collarbone.

She trembled under his touch, her fingers sliding beneath his shirt, seeking skin.

He shucked it off, impatient now. She ran her hands across his chest, pausing when she reached the scar just beneath his ribs.

"How did you get this?" she asked, her voice barely above a breath.

"Motorcycle accident. I was seventeen. Thought I was invincible."

She looked up at him, her brow drawn. "You're not?"

His lips twitched. "No. I'm not."

"Well, that bursts one bubble. I guess you can die from pleasure then," she teased.

Their eyes met—raw and unguarded—and something shifted.

For him, this wasn't just lust.

This was her giving him everything—and trusting that he would protect the gift she was offering.

He reached for her again, lifting her gently as he slid off her panties, letting them fall to the side before stripping the rest of his clothes.

And then he paused.

She lay there, wide-eyed, her cheeks flushed, her chest rising and falling with anticipation and nerves. She was an offering to the Gods, her hair a silk curtain of black with fire threading through—like her kisses.

Theo's heart thudded against his ribs. He reached for the drawer beside the bed, pulled out protection, and then knelt beside her, stroking her hair back from her face.

"Still okay?" he asked.

She nodded. "Yes, but getting a little impatient. I didn't realize it took so long. There's a part of me that wants to throw you down and have its wicked way with you before I self-combust."

He chuckled and licked the tip of her nipple, causing her to gasp and bow. "And the other part?"

"The other part—" She paused, her voice shaking. "The other part wants to see what you do."

"How about we do that first? Then you can have your wicked way with me," he suggested, tweaking her other nipple until she was breathing in gasps and crying out his name.

Theo took his time, letting his hands and lips reassure her, teach her. There was no rush, only reverence. He kissed her jaw, her throat, her shoulder, trailing warmth down her body until she arched into him, her eyes fluttering closed.

"I'm going to taste every inch of you. By the time I'm done, no one else will ever compare. No other man will ever be able to touch you the way I do. Make you come the way I will. Tell me what you want, Rose."

"You... I want... you," she breathed out.

"Keep your hands above your head," he ordered.

Her dazed eyes stared back at him. "But... why? I want to touch you."

"Later. For now, this is about you and your pleasure. I'll let you know when you can touch me," he promised.

He knew if she touched him now, with the way she was reacting to him, and the way his body was on fire, that he wouldn't be able to go slow. He didn't want to hurt her. She was petite. He... well, he knew he was well-endowed.

"Well, it shouldn't take long," she panted as he moved down her body and parted her legs.

"Oh, my! Oh-oh-oh!" she cried out, her body jolting and bucking when he moved between her parted thighs.

Theo loved how responsive she was to his touch. He caressed her sensitive nub, teasing it with his fingers, his tongue, his lips, until she was crying wildly and trying to pull away. He loved that she kept her fingers wrapped around the decorative bars of his headboard.

The emotions flashing across her face, the way her lips parted when he hit an especially sensitive spot, the way her breasts swayed as she twisted and bucked, turned him on harder than he had ever been in his life.

She stiffened when he slid a finger into her vaginal canal. He gently lapped at her until she moaned and relaxed with pleasure. She began moving; rocking her hips when he slid two fingers into her so he could gently stretch her.

"That's it. Take it, *kardiá mou*," he encouraged, pressing as deep as he could until he felt the thin barrier.

"Theo… please… I need—"

Her gasps turned to soft moans when he gently stroked her, increasing the friction. Her fingers clenched the headboard, her head thrown back, her lips parted on a guttural cry as she came.

Theo rose over her, caging her. He tore the condom open with his teeth, discarded the foil, and rolled it over his throbbing shaft, gritting his teeth at the sensitivity.

With a coarse curse, he fitted himself to her ready channel and entered her with infinite care. She tensed—but only for a breath—and then relaxed beneath him, releasing the headboard so she could slide her hands up his chest as he stilled.

Her lips parted on a breathy, "Theo…"

"Oh, *agápi mou*. You are so beautiful."

He groaned her name like a prayer, kissing her temple, whispering praise as they began moving in unison.

He kept his focus on her face, measuring her responses as he rocked his hips, pressing deeper with each thrust.

She was driving him crazy, and he knew he wouldn't last long. He'd never in his life tried so hard to keep from coming.

The feel of his cock sliding in and out of her sent spirals of exquisite pleasure through him until it was almost painful. He knew he wasn't going to last much longer when the familiar tingling built and his balls tightened harder than he'd ever been before.

He held nothing back. His control frayed with each breath, each whisper, each connection of skin to skin. When she came apart beneath him again, gasping his name, quivering in his arms, he followed—his release crashing over him with a force that left him shuddering with pleasure.

What had just happened between them literally took his breath away.

"My Rose. My beautiful Rose," he breathed, wrapping his arms around her and holding her as tightly as he could without crushing her.

His mind was spinning out of control. His cock, still buried inside her, twitched as the last of his orgasm slowly faded. He cursed the condom —grateful for it, yet furious at the distance it put between them.

An image blindsided him—Rose, glowing, rounded with his child. The thought was so foreign, it stunned him. He'd never pictured a future like that—until now.

*Where the hell did that thought come from?*

He breathed, knowing he needed to care for Rose, but he didn't want to move. Hell, he wasn't sure if he could! His bones felt as if they had melted. The thought amused him because that was another first for him.

"What's so funny?" Rose asked, peering at him with a suspicious expression.

He kissed her, caressing her lips with his before he replied.

"I need to take care of you—" he said, gazing down at her.

She sniffed, her fingers curling against his shoulders. He had the feeling she was about to push him away. He tightened his arms around her and bent to whisper in her ear.

"—but you've melted my bones to the point I'm not sure I can move."

"Oh... Oh!" She giggled and began caressing his shoulders with her fingertips while moving her hips. "Then, laugh away while I continue working on my devious plan of committing death by pleasure."

"I would die a very happy man," he teased, capturing her swollen lips again.

# Ten

Theo closed his eyes and counted to ten.

It didn't work.

*Give her a moment. Let her enjoy a shower. You know what will happen if you get in it with her,* he scolded himself.

He groaned when his body disagreed. He glared at his wayward cock that was already tenting the jogging pants he had pulled on.

"You're not helping," he muttered to the lower half of his body.

Rose, bare beneath the streaming water, burned in his mind like molten gold. His fleeting chivalry died a hasty death.

"I agree, she should pick out what she wants to eat."

He gave up the pretense of trying to resist, turned, and retraced his path to his bedroom.

He entered the bathroom to find a goddess shrouded in steam.

Through the clouded glass, Rose's silhouette moved with a grace that stopped his breath. He pushed the loose jogging pants off his lean hips, kicked them to the side, and made a beeline for the shower.

The door slid open on a wave of heat. Rose looked over her shoulder, her eyes lighting in welcome and her lips parting with promise.

She reached for him, her small hand closing around his aching shaft in a touch that was both possessive and reverent. Her fingers flexed.

"Come here," she murmured, tugging him inside. "It took you long enough to come back."

Pleasure punched through him, sharp and immediate. He crowded her against the wall, letting the warm spray soak his hair and run down his back.

Her lips brushed his chest, soft and teasing. She tweaked his nipples with her tongue before she began a slow descent down his body.

Theo's breath left him in a harsh groan.

Before she could kneel, he caught her wrists, pulling her back up and pinning her hands above her head. The move made her laugh, the sound low and throaty in the confined space.

He was about to claim her mouth when his gaze fell on a small mark just inside the bend of her elbow.

He cupped her wrists in one hand and brushed the water from his eyes, frowning. Leaning closer, he studied the birthmark.

Water slid over the faint shape. Italy; the boot, even Sicily.

His grip tightened as he felt a sudden, brutal twist in his chest.

"What is this?" he asked roughly, his thumb brushing the outline.

She tilted her head, the corners of her lips curving. "A birthmark. My grandmother said my mother had the same one. Why?"

Her teasing tone barely registered. Theo swallowed hard, his mind churning.

No. Impossible. And yet, the shape…

Mother and daughter… her last name…

It was too much of a coincidence.

She wiggled her nose at him. "If you don't let me go, I'm going to shrivel into a prune before we get anything to eat. For some reason, I'm suddenly starving!"

He caressed the mark once more before he kissed her and forced himself to release her, schooling his face into something close to normal.

"I'll feed you," he promised, though his voice came out low and uneven.

She rewarded him with a smile and rose on her toes to kiss him, warm and unguarded, before slipping beneath his arm and stepping out of the shower with a playful slap on his right buttock and a giggle.

He stood there for a moment, water streaming down his body, while his world tilted on its axis.

By the time he turned off the taps and stepped out, she was wrapped in a towel, already disappearing toward the bedroom. "I'll be in the kitchen," she called.

He reached for his own towel—but his gaze snagged on the bathroom counter.

Her silver locket sat there, delicate and unassuming.

He picked it up.

The weight of it was light in his palm, but something deep inside him felt heavy. He caressed the seam with his thumbnail before applying pressure.

The locket snapped open. For a split second, guilt pierced him—he'd opened what wasn't his. But the guilt drowned beneath the tidal wave of certainty.

Lost in the shock of his discovery, he didn't notice the tiny scrap of color that slipped free and fell to the tile. His attention was locked on the two smiling faces inside.

The image of the dark-haired woman with Rose's mouth struck him in the gut. He knew her face as if it were his own. He had been studying it for the past three months.

Livia Alliata.

The air left his lungs in a curse. He braced a hand on the counter, his hip digging into the edge as the room seemed to spin.

It couldn't be.

But… it was.

*Rose… my Rose… is Livia's daughter.*

The thought echoed through his mind.

He had found Lorenzo and Sophia's missing granddaughter. She was his lover.

He closed the locket, his hand tightening around it. The ripple of realization cut both ways—one part shock, one part something far more dangerous.

This changed everything.

Not only had he found her… he'd crossed a line there was no coming back from.

He had touched her, claimed her, wanted her in ways that went far beyond the boundaries of his godfather's trust.

And yet—

No, he hadn't betrayed Lorenzo's trust. This only made things inevitable.

His gaze slid through the open bathroom door to the rumpled sheets where she'd lain with him only minutes ago. He wasn't going to lose her. If anything, this made his course of action clearer.

Tomorrow, he'd call Mimi. He'd tell her Rose needed to be free of the theatre. That she needed to come with him to London.

He would need to arrange a DNA test—it would just be a formality, undeniable proof for Lorenzo and Sophia's protection—but he already knew what the results would be.

Rose was Livia's daughter.

Which meant Lorenzo wasn't just about to gain a granddaughter, he was going to gain a new grandson-in-law.

Theo wasn't going to let anything—past, present, or future—stand in the way of that.

"Hey, are you okay?" Rose asked, pulling him out of his daze.

"What? Yes. I'll be right there," he said, closing his hand over the locket and bending to retrieve the jogging pants he had discarded minutes ago.

"Okay. I wasn't sure if you had fallen asleep in the shower," she teased.

His gaze softened. She looked so beautiful wearing his dress shirt from earlier and nothing else. A fierce sense of protectiveness swept through him. His beautiful Rose's life was about to change—drastically—in a very short amount of time.

"Let's eat, then I think we should get some sleep," he suggested.

She laughed, turned, and gave him a sexy smile over her shoulder. "Considering it is almost three in the morning, I agree. I'm going to be part of New York's walking dead tomorrow. But, God! What a way to go. Oh, I think I heard the microwave ping. I call dibs on the first round."

He pulled on his jogging pants and chuckled when she twirled and disappeared. He paused again, picked up his cellphone, and shot a quick text to Nikos.

*Need to see you first thing in the morning.*

*Yeah, same. See you early.*

"Theo, dinner!" Rose called from the kitchen.

"Coming."

"You will once you see what is for dessert," she replied.

Theo laughed and shook his head. He replaced his phone on the nightstand and headed for the door.

"Yes, my lovely Rose. Life is about to get very interesting," he murmured with growing excitement.

The low, insistent vibration of a phone pulled her from the edges of sleep. She reached blindly across the bed, her fingers brushing over cool sheets instead of warm skin. Her eyes blinked open to the soft gray light of dawn.

Theo's side of the bed was empty.

Somewhere beyond the bedroom door, the shower ran in a steady, distant rhythm. She squinted at the clock on the nightstand. Six o'clock. Barely.

Groaning, she rolled over, dragging his pillow against her chest. The scent of him—clean soap, warm skin, and a faint thread of something darker and masculine—wrapped around her, and she buried her face in it.

God, she was tired.

Every inch of her felt tender, in the best possible way. Her lips still tingled from his kisses, her body thrummed with the echo of his touch. She hadn't known it was possible to make love so many creative ways —slow and reverent, fast and desperate, playful, teasing, and everything in between. The memories sent a traitorous flicker of heat spiraling through her belly.

The bathroom door opened, releasing a wave of steam into the bedroom.

Theo stepped out, dressed in charcoal slacks and a crisp white shirt, his hair still damp. Even this early, he looked like he was about to close a million-dollar deal.

She peeked up from the pillow, a happy smile curving her lips. "Where are you going at this hour?" she asked, her voice husky with sleep.

"Nikos is on his way over," he said, leaning down to brush his lips across her forehead. "We need to discuss a few things. It shouldn't take long."

She groaned and dropped back against the pillows. "It's barely morning."

His fingers slid through her hair, pushing it back from her face in a touch so tender it made her chest ache. "Sleep in," he murmured.

She nodded, the soft pillow molding to her cheek as he left. She listened to his footsteps, a faint whisper against the plush carpet. The muffled click of the closing bedroom door brought a sigh to her lips.

She lay there, eyes closed, desperately trying to recapture the peace of sleep, but her traitorous mind was wide awake. She was accustomed to the theatre's early mornings, to the expectant hum of tasks waiting to unfold. Despite the deliciously boneless, almost melting feel of her body, the thought of the empty stage tugged at her, a hollow echo in her mind.

With a sigh, she pushed the covers back and swung her legs over the side of the bed. She quickly made the bed before she gathered her discarded clothes from the night before.

She padded into the bathroom, breathing in the fresh scent of Theo's aftershave. With a low groan of pleasure, she turned on the shower. The warm water washed away the lingering ache in her muscles, but the heat only seemed to sharpen the awareness still humming through her.

She stepped out, pulled the towel off the rack, and dried off. Humming a show tune under her breath, she wrapped the towel around her, found Theo's comb, and bent at the waist to brush her damp hair out. She was rising again when a speck of green on the white tile caught her eye.

Frowning, she bent and plucked it up. Her breath caught as she realized what it was. It was a tiny, perfectly pressed four-leaf clover.

The clover had been in her locket since childhood—a charm from her grandfather, never removed. She straightened slowly, the damp air feeling suddenly too heavy against her skin.

Her gaze slid to the counter. She had left her locket there last night, before they'd stepped into the shower together. It was gone.

Rose frowned. She searched the bathroom floor, the drawers, even the laundry basket, thinking it might have gotten tangled up by mistake. Nothing.

She gently fingered the clover. The only way it could have fallen out was if the locket had been opened.

*Maybe Theo's curious. Maybe he has it.*

She pulled the towel free and dressed. She would ask him if he had seen it. Her fingers went to her neck out of habit. She turned, catching her reflection in the mirror. Her expression softened. She didn't know if she looked different now—but she felt it.

"Everything will be alright. He didn't leave you because he didn't like what happened. It wasn't just a one-night stand," she whispered, staring at her reflection.

*And if it was?* her bad side asked.

"If it was, then that is all you were going to give him anyway," she replied, knowing it was a lie.

She sighed and turned away. She'd find Theo. His reaction would reveal if her trust had been a mistake or a gift.

Theo stood in front of the wall of windows in his living room, staring at the faint color of sunlight rising on the horizon.

Sleep had been an illusion after his discovery that Rose and Livia's child were one and the same. Even with Rose curled into him, her breathing slow and even, her warmth seeping into his skin… his mind hadn't stopped—nor had his feelings of guilt. He told himself his plans were for her protection—that she needed him, even if she didn't see it yet.

He'd tried over dinner to steer the conversation toward her parents. She had shrugged and said there wasn't much to talk about, as they had died when she was only a month old.

When she had asked about his family instead, he'd redirected her back to her grandparents, hoping to glean a morsel of information about Livia. He listened as she painted vivid pictures of backstage mishaps, eccentric directors, and Mimi's close encounters with the artists who had performed there over the years.

He'd laughed—really laughed—but beneath the humor, the birthmark burned in his thoughts like an ember that refused to go out.

Later, she'd driven him mad again in the bedroom, stripping away any hope of keeping a clear head. And then she'd fallen asleep in his arms, soft and utterly trusting, while he lay awake in the dark, tracing the mark on her arm, thinking of Livia.

His plan was already forming—solid, immovable.

He would take her home.

Markos or Nikos could handle the London and Paris meetings. He'd take Rome and Athens himself. That would give him weeks with her. Weeks to help her settle into his world, meet his family, stand beside him as his.

They would marry as soon as possible.

A darker thought slipped in. After, the second time they'd made love tonight, he'd noticed a tear in the condom. Likely his fault—too impatient, too eager. He'd discarded it without a word. It wasn't the time to tell her.

He turned when a soft knock, followed by the quiet click of the door opening, pulled him from his thoughts.

Nikos stepped in, his sharp eyes scanning the room like a man who noticed everything. His gaze paused on the pair of delicate heels left in the foyer, then on Theo's jacket draped casually over the armrest. His eyebrow arched in silent question.

Theo gave a small, deliberate nod.

Nikos exhaled slowly, the sound equal parts resignation and understanding. Without a word, he tilted his head toward the office.

They walked in; leaving the door slightly ajar in their distraction. Theo moved to the windows, the city stretching out below in a glittering sprawl, his back to Nikos.

For a long moment, there was only the hum of the building and their breaths.

When Nikos finally spoke, his voice carried the weight of something carefully chosen.

"I got a message. From Warren Roberts—the oldest son of the old woman who used to live next to Chris. He lives on the West Coast and didn't respond until the wee hours here."

Theo's shoulders stiffened. "Go on."

"He remembered the couple from years ago because he used to hang out with Chris Smythe." Nikos stepped closer, his voice steady but quieter now. "He said Chris met a young woman from Italy… a beautiful woman named Livia. He didn't remember her last name. She came over on a visa to attend Juilliard."

Theo turned slightly, his pulse a slow, heavy thud in his chest.

"According to Warren, Chris and Livia fell hard for each other. Warren was there when they eloped. Livia was three months pregnant. She hid it. According to what Chris told Warren, Livia's parents never would've approved of him, especially with them both being so young. Chris told Warren Livia's parents had other plans for her—someone else she was supposed to marry. But Chris adored her… and their daughter when she came along."

The words landed like blows. Each one cemented what Theo already knew in his bones.

Nikos's voice softened, tinged with something like grief.

"A month after the baby's birth, on the drive home from a Medieval Arts Festival, a semi blew a tire in bad weather. Livia died instantly, along with two others. Chris..." Nikos's throat worked. "Chris was left in a vegetative state."

Theo stared at the city lights, each point of brightness blurring at the edges.

"Warren lost touch with the grandparents after that," Nikos went on quietly. "But he saw Chris's obituary five years later."

The silence that followed was heavy enough to press into Theo's chest.

Nikos moved closer, placing a hand on his shoulder—a small gesture of solidarity in the storm gathering inside him.

Theo lowered his gaze, his other hand closing around the locket in his pocket. He pulled it free and placed it in Nikos's palm.

Nikos flipped it open. His eyebrows rose at the photograph, then he gave a low, knowing whistle. "So this is why you've been looking like a man caught between heaven and hell."

Theo's voice was low, hard with certainty. "We'll need to get a DNA sample from Rose to confirm it, but I know she's Livia's daughter."

Nikos studied the tiny image of Livia, her smile frozen in time, then shut the locket with a quiet snap. "I didn't realize she looked so much like Livia."

Theo nodded once, the motion short, final.

Nikos's mouth quirked in something between irony and awe. "Sometimes it's a small world."

Theo's gaze turned inward, the truth of it pulsing in his blood. Small world... and getting smaller. Because there was no way in hell he was letting Rose slip out of his arms now—not when she was his in every way that mattered.

The cool marble chilled her bare feet as she padded out of the bedroom, careful not to make a sound. She hadn't meant to eavesdrop —only to pass quietly through the living room and find something to drink—but Nikos's voice stopped her mid-step.

"…Chris Smythe…"

Her breath caught.

Her father's name.

Every instinct told her to walk away. Instead, she drifted toward the partially closed door, each step drawn by an invisible thread until she stood just outside his office.

Nikos was speaking now, his deep voice steady, clinical, almost like a storyteller recounting someone else's tragedy. But the story he was telling… was hers.

She leaned in, the words hitting her in pieces—Livia, Juilliard, eloped, pregnant. A medieval festival. The truck. The accident.

Her fingers curled against the doorframe for support.

Her mother. Her father.

She wanted to cry out, to demand how they even knew these things, but shock pinned her in place.

"…Lorenzo will want to know as soon as it can be confirmed," Nikos finished.

Her knees wobbled. *Lorenzo?*

Her grandmother had told her—clear as day—that Lorenzo and Sophia Alliata had wanted nothing to do with her. They had told her grandparents that it would have been better if she had never been born.

Her stomach churned at the thought of meeting them now—after all these years.

"So, what's next... now that you've found her?" Nikos asked.

Theo spoke, his voice calm, deliberate. "I'll contact Mimi Devan later this morning and tell her that if the theatre wants a charitable donation, she'll have to terminate Rose's living and working arrangements. Immediately."

Rose's head snapped up, disbelief slicing through the haze.

"She'll have no choice but to depend on me," Theo continued smoothly. "I'll take her first to Greece. We'll marry there. Then to Italy —where I'll introduce her to her grandparents."

Marry? Greece? Italy?

Her heart pounded in her ears as Nikos asked, "How do you think your godfather's going to handle the fact that you married his granddaughter without asking first?"

Theo didn't hesitate. "He'll approve. It would be the perfect merger between our families."

Rose bit her lip when there was a lull in their conversation, as if both men were deep in their own thoughts.

Nikos wryly continued. "How do you think Rose will feel about her sudden engagement?"

"She'll accept it. I told you it was inevitable—especially after last night," Theo replied. The cold certainty in his tone made her skin prickle. "What other choice would she have once she no longer has the theatre to hide in? She has no other family. She'll have no job. No place to live. And... there's a possibility she could be pregnant. The condom broke."

The air left her lungs in a sharp, soundless gasp.

"Besides, what woman do you know would who turn down being the granddaughter of Italian nobility—and marrying a billionaire?" Theo asked.

Nikos snorted out a laugh. "When you asked me that same question before, I wasn't thinking of Rose. But... knowing her, I wouldn't place any bets on it until you get a ring on her finger—or at least get her on a plane heading to Greece."

Her gaze landed on Nikos's hand when he waved at Theo through the crack in the door.

He was holding her locket.

The floor seemed to tilt.

Heat flooded her face—not from embarrassment, but from a white-hot fury that made her fingers tremble.

Without a sound, she backed away from the door. The surrounding room blurred, her body moving on instinct as she slipped into the living room and grabbed her purse, shoes, and shawl.

It wasn't Theo's words that gutted her—it was the cool certainty in his voice. The warmth she had fallen for was gone, replaced by calculation. As if she were just another business deal for him—one he'd made with her mother's parents.

By the time she reached the elevator, her resolve had crystallized into steel.

She wasn't a delicate bloom that needed Theo Kallistratos—or anyone —to save her.

Mimi would absolutely accept the terms of Theo's donation. Her first thought would be the theatre—not to the girl who did maintenance.

That was fine.

What Theo didn't realize was that she had her own resources. Her grandfather had left her enough to live comfortably. Plus, she had her degree. She could always find another job.

She stepped into the elevator and pulled her phone from her purse, her hand shaking so badly she nearly dropped it.

Kerry picked up on the third ring, her voice muffled with sleep. "Rose? It's barely—"

A choked sob ripped from Rose's throat before she could speak.

"Hey, what's wrong?" Kerry's voice sharpened instantly, all sleep gone.

Rose swallowed hard, the words scraping her throat. "Has your brother left yet?"

"No… we were out late last night. Why?"

Rose closed her eyes, inhaling shakily. "Would he… be interested in a little company on his trip back to Nebraska?"

There was a beat of silence, and then Kerry's voice softened. "Oh, sweetheart…" She murmured something low and fierce that Rose didn't catch, then said, "I'll meet you at the theatre in half an hour."

Rose nodded even though Kerry couldn't see it. "Thank you." Her voice cracked.

She ended the call before the tears could fall.

By the time the cab pulled from the curb, her jaw was set and her gaze was fixed on the bright ribbon of asphalt ahead—a road she would choose, not one Theo carved for her.

Theo thought she had no choice. But she did. And she was about to take it.

# Eleven

An hour later, Theo walked beside Nikos toward the private entrance of the penthouse. He was thinking about how quickly he could get Mimi on the phone, about the arrangements that would need to be made—when Nikos stopped abruptly.

"What is it?"

Nikos's gaze swept the space, his frown deepening. "Where are her shoes? They were here when I came in."

The question hit like a blow. Theo's stomach turned to stone. Her purse, shoes, and shawl were gone.

He cursed, strode down the hall, and pushed open the bedroom door.

The sight of her clothes gone—the bed made—hit harder than any hostile takeover. Rose wasn't just gone, it was like she'd erased herself, and their night together.

An icy thread of dread wound through his spine.

Behind him, Nikos's voice was low but pointed. "Do you think she could have overheard us?"

Theo bowed his head, closed his eyes, and visualized the scene from earlier. Despair rose inside him as his gaze locked on his office door.

If she'd been standing close enough… if she'd heard everything—

"*Gamóto!*" Damn it! The curse tore from him as the truth twisted his stomach. "She heard us… and she's gone."

Theo's jaw flexed. He yanked his phone out of his pocket and called the front desk.

The concierge answered promptly. "Good morning, Mr. Kallistratos."

"A young woman, early-twenties, wearing a pale blue dress—did you see her leave?"

"Yes, sir. She exited about forty-five minutes ago."

Theo ended the call, shoving the phone into his pocket with another muttered curse. The coil of frustration inside him twisted tighter.

"I don't even have her number," he said flatly, as if admitting a tactical oversight in a deal.

"I've got her friend Kerry's," Nikos offered.

Theo took it without hesitation, already punching in the digits. The call rang once—twice—before dropping into voicemail.

"Kerry, this is Theo Kallistratos," he said, his voice hard-edged with control he didn't feel. "It's urgent you call me back. It's about Rose."

He hung up and strode toward the door. Nikos fell into step beside him.

"She'll go back to the theatre—it's the only place she feels safe. I have to reach her before she decides I'm a bigger bastard than she already thinks I am."

They exited the penthouse, the elevator doors sliding shut with a metallic finality that only sharpened the pressure in his chest.

*She has to listen,* he thought with a growing sense of panic. *I'm not letting her walk out of my life. Not without a fight.*

Rose zipped the last pocket of her backpack and exhaled a slow, shaky breath. Everything she owned worth taking fit inside it. Her carry-on held the keepsakes she couldn't leave—programs, her grandfather's watch, old letters, her grandmother's scarf, and on top, a photo of the two of them smiling.

Her fingers lingered on the glass, tracing the lines of his familiar face.

*You'd know what to do, Pop.* She blinked against the sting in her eyes. *You always did.*

She zipped the carry-on before she walked over to the kitchenette table. She placed an envelope addressed to Mimi on it. The letter inside was short: she quit, and she was gone. Beside it, she placed the theatre keys, the cold metal feeling heavier than they should in her palm before she let them go.

By the time Kerry arrived, Rose had her coat on and was tightening the straps of her backpack. Kerry didn't ask questions. She just crossed the small space in two strides and wrapped her in a hug that smelled faintly of coffee and floral shampoo.

Rose tried for a smile, but it wavered at the corners. "I'm ready."

Kerry gave a small nod, her eyes warm but shadowed with unspoken concern. "Robby's waiting at the loading dock. He'll swing me by my place, but he's eager to get on the road."

"Thank you." Her voice was thick. "I'll explain everything... I just can't right now."

"You don't have to," Kerry said softly, giving her hand a squeeze that was both a promise and a lifeline. "I've got your back. So does Robby."

Rose swallowed hard against the lump in her throat. Kerry picked up the carry-on and together they slipped out through the back.

The chilly morning air hit her cheeks as they stepped onto the loading dock. Robby stood by the idling truck, leaning against the door with his arms crossed. His eyes softened when he saw her.

"Hey, it's good to meet you finally," he said simply, taking the bags from them without another word. He placed them in the back of the truck while she and Kerry climbed in the cab.

Minutes later, the truck was rumbling through the thin, early-morning traffic. New York slid past in a blur of gray and gold, the sun just starting to edge over the skyline.

When Robby pulled up in front of Kerry's apartment, Rose climbed out so her friend could slide from the cab. Kerry caught her in another hug, holding on tight.

"Promise me you'll call when you can."

Rose nodded, the motion small.

Kerry's eyes narrowed slightly. "I'm assuming this has to do with the billionaire."

"He turned out to be a toad, not a prince," she said, the words brittle. "Better to find out before I fell in love."

She knew Kerry could see through the lie. It was there in the way her friend's eyes softened, in the way she pressed her lips together but didn't call her out.

"Stay strong," Kerry said firmly. "Keep in touch. And if the toad calls, I'll tell him to hop straight into a boiling pot."

A reluctant, strained laugh escaped Rose. "Deal." She hugged Kerry one last time, breathing her in like she might never see her again, then climbed back into the truck.

The city faded behind them within minutes, swallowed by the highway. Rose stared out the window, her heart aching with each passing mile, Theo's betrayal slicing through the thorny wall she'd always used to protect her heart.

Her fingers drifted to her throat before she remembered—there was no locket there anymore. Theo had taken it. Her vision blurred, but she blinked the tears back. She had other pictures of her parents. She'd make a new locket.

Her hand slipped to her left arm, rubbing absently over the birthmark beneath the sleeve of her coat. She focused on the steady motion, grounding herself in the feel of the knit and the muted hum of the road beneath the truck tires.

Time and distance, that was the cure. *Time for the wound to scab and distance to keep Theo Kallistratos from ever finding me again.*

She kept her eyes fixed on the horizon until the skyline disappeared completely, willing her heart to harden. This was her fresh start—and she'd burn every bridge to keep it.

Three days.

Three infuriating, sleepless, gut-twisting days since Rose had vanished without a trace. From the moment she slipped out, he'd been ready to strangle himself for letting her get away. Now the frustration had hardened into a gnawing impatience.

Her friend Kerry had been no help.

When Kerry had finally answered one of his calls, she'd greeted him in a tone dripping with false sweetness: *'Why don't you jump in a pot of boiling water—oh, and while you're at it, drop dead. I can put the pot on the stove if you'd like.'*

Then she hung up and blocked his number.

Nikos had laughed for a solid thirty seconds when Theo told him. Theo didn't think it was nearly as funny.

Mimi had eventually, reluctantly, given up Rose's phone number. Not that it mattered—every call went straight to voicemail. Every message, unanswered.

He stood at the window now, his jaw tight, the city sprawling endlessly beneath him. He had London and Paris meetings he should have been attending this week, but Nikos had handed those off to his twin, Markos, so he could stay here and focus on what actually mattered—finding Rose.

The sound of the office door opening pulled him from his thoughts. Nikos strolled in like a man returning from a holiday, not three days of hunting a missing woman.

"What have you found?" Theo asked.

Nikos held up a folder. "Special delivery."

Theo pivoted, his hand snapping out to take it. Inside, a neatly clipped report waited. His eyes landed on the heading, his pulse thudding harder as he flipped it open.

**DNA Results.**

The breath he pulled in was slow and deliberate, as though steadying himself before a fight. The familiar ache of anticipation tightened in his chest. A sample of Rose's blood, taken when she nicked her finger in the kitchen and discarded her Band-Aid before her shower, had been enough to confirm what he already knew in his bones—Rose was Livia's daughter.

He closed his eyes for a moment, his head bowed over the file. The proof should have brought him peace. Instead, it brought fire— because the woman he'd betrayed was the very one he'd been searching for all along.

When he looked up again, Nikos was lounging in the chair opposite him, legs stretched out like a man without a care in the world and a smug smile pulling at his mouth.

"What the hell are you so happy about? This doesn't change the fact that she's disappeared," Theo asked, his tone sharper than intended.

Nikos nodded toward the folder. "Keep reading."

Theo's brow furrowed as he turned the page—and froze. A grainy traffic cam image stared back at him, a box truck caught mid-frame. The words Evans Classic Furniture were stenciled across the side in bold script, along with a colorful design that looked like custom-made furnishings. A phone number and location: Nebraska.

"What does this have to do with Rose?" he demanded.

Nikos stretched his arms overhead, catlike, and grinned. "Kerry's last name is Evans." He jabbed a finger toward the picture. "That's her brother's business. He owns a custom furniture store outside of Omaha. That shot was taken three days ago, right outside Kerry's apartment."

Theo's fingers tightened around the page. "Where's the rest?"

"Ah," Nikos drawled, the sound stretching like he had all the time in the world. "Go on. Turn the page. You'll like this."

Theo did—and his breath caught. Another image, this one clearer, closer. Two women embracing on the sidewalk. One of them—hair falling over her shoulder, face tilted up in a sad smile—was Rose.

Nikos leaned back, utterly pleased with himself. "Cost us a couple VIP tickets to the club and the promise of a blind date with the traffic controller's sister, but if it works out, it was worth it."

Theo's eyes never left the photograph. "Can we prove she left with him?"

Nikos's grin faltered into something more sheepish. He sat forward, resting his elbows on his knees. "Maybe."

"Maybe?"

"I might have… encouraged a friend to make a call."

Theo gave him a flat look.

"Sherry Contessa. You know—the more dangerous twin."

Theo groaned.

"She pretended to be from the theatre," Nikos went on, far too casually. "Called Robby Evans's mother and asked if Rose was there yet. Belinda Evans said they should be arriving by tomorrow. Sherry said she'd call back in a few days."

Theo's breath hissed out. His eyes glittered with purpose as he reached for his phone.

"Schedule me a flight to Omaha," he told his PA when she answered. "And arrange transportation."

He'd barely ended the call when his phone pinged. A message from Lorenzo.

*Did you receive the report?*

"Lorenzo already knows?" he asked, standing when Nikos stood.

Nikos shrugged. "The minute you asked for the DNA test, he suspected you'd found her. He's impatient to meet her. By the way, I'll meet you at the airport," Nikos added.

Theo raised a brow. "Why?"

"Because until you get Rose on a plane to Greece, you're not out of the woods," Nikos replied with a laugh.

Theo's lips curved despite himself. "Fair point."

"Plus, Markos and I have a bet," Nikos called over his shoulder as he left.

"About what?"

Nikos's grin was pure Cheshire Cat—smug, knowing, infuriating. "Which one of you admits you're in love first."

Theo chuckled quietly as Nikos lifted a hand in farewell before he strolled out the door. Theo shook his head. He already knew who would admit it first—him.

*If Rose gives me a chance*, he thought ruefully.

His lips curved when his phone pinged again. Lorenzo was impatient. His grin sharpened as he lifted the phone to his ear.

Everything revolved around Rose. And this time, he wasn't letting her slip through his fingers.

"Lorenzo, you received the report," he greeted.

# Twelve

Rose could tell from the tight set of Robby's jaw that she'd officially driven him to the brink of his patience.

Well… parked herself at the brink, technically, since the van she wanted wasn't hers yet.

*But it will be!*

Over the last two days on the road, she'd learned a few things about Kerry's older brother:

First: he treated speed limit signs like vague suggestions from a friend he didn't trust.

Second: he had a low, easy drawl that could probably sell furniture to a cat.

Third: he was developing more than a passing interest in her.

And while she appreciated him—and adored his sister—her heart was still a smoking crater thanks to Theo Kallistratos. Which meant she had exactly zero emotional bandwidth for another man—even one as nice as Robby Evans.

That was why she'd been scrolling on her phone earlier, searching for a way to let him down gently, when it appeared.

The ad.

The glorious, destiny-altering, *'I'm about to live in a van down by the river,'* ad.

Now, they were standing in front of a cheerful little house in Fort Smith, Arkansas, arguing about it like an old married couple—minus the ring, the romance, and the shared Netflix password.

"I'm not saying it's not a good deal," Robby argued, rubbing the back of his neck. "I'm saying… why the rush? Why not just come to Omaha, stay with me for a while? Let me help you get settled before you—" he gestured at the driveway like it was a crime scene, "—buy a tiny hippy van and go live God knows where."

Rose pressed her lips together to keep from grinning. "It's not a hippie van."

"It's got daisies, peace signs, and paw prints on it, Rose," he replied in a dry voice.

"That's called personality."

"It's called 'arrested at the border for suspicious floral activity'—not to mention you'll get pulled over at every county line to see if you are smoking weed."

She crossed her arms. "You just don't understand. This isn't just any van—it's a 1990 VW Westfalia. Low miles. Rebuilt engine—by a certified mechanic for his *daughter*—plus a gorgeous paint job. It's basically a unicorn with a carburetor."

Robby gave her a look. "It's a magnet for trouble. If you want a car, I can help you find one when we get to Omaha. There's no reason for you to worry about needing to find a place right away. Mom and Dad's house is huge. You can stay in Kerry's room."

Rose bit her lip. She could hear the *or mine* that he wanted to add but didn't.

"I'll come—for a few days. I mean… it might be nice to have a place to outfit the van and… get better at driving, from someone who knows what they're doing."

His eyebrows rose. "Get better at driving?"

She shifted her weight from one foot to the other. "I have my license."

"That's not what I asked."

Her voice went small. "There was no reason to drive back home. Okay… I've only driven once—to pass my test."

His blink was slow. "Once? That's it?"

"I lived in the city! You don't need a car there. You just need comfortable shoes, a decent sense of direction, and public transit."

Robby groaned like a man picturing his own funeral arrangements. "Great. I hope you know that Kerry's going to skin me alive."

Rose grinned. "She'll boil you in oil first to make it easier."

A short while later, the deal was done, the keys were in her hand, and she was floating somewhere between terror and giddy triumph. She had a home and transportation. All she needed now was a job… and maybe a magician who could wipe out the last month of her memory.

The van was unapologetically ridiculous—flowers, peace signs, and paw prints scattered like confetti. The seller had explained it was a refurbished college graduation gift for his oldest daughter. Three months ago, she had married a doctor and moved to California, leaving the van behind like a perfectly painted orphan.

Now it was Rose's.

Two hours later, she was following Robby's big truck down the highway, gripping the steering wheel like it was a lifeline and giving herself pep talks out loud.

"You're fine. Totally fine. The lane lines are your friends. The semi next to you is not trying to eat you."

The van hummed beneath her, smelling faintly of old leather, new vinyl, and maybe… optimism?

But as the road stretched out ahead, her mind circled back to Theo and Nikos's conversation, the words still cutting like glass. Her chest ached, but she focused on the ridiculous fact that she was piloting a psychedelic van toward Nebraska like some heartbroken Scooby-Doo extra.

This wasn't running. This was moving forward—one psychedelic mile at a time.

~

Theo's jaw ached from grinding his teeth.

They'd been in Nebraska for all of two hours, and in that time, the GPS had tried to murder them twice— once down a cow path, and again at an abandoned grain silo with rusted tracks. Both times with a cheerful *'You have arrived'*.

Now, finally, the correct mailbox loomed into view, the numbers painted in neat black script. Theo exhaled a long, slow breath, the kind meant to purge a man's frustration before it turned homicidal.

"Turn here," he said.

Nikos swung the rental SUV onto the winding drive, the tires crunching over gravel. A box truck sat in front of a sprawling white farmhouse with a wraparound porch, Evans Classic Furniture stenciled across its side in old-fashioned lettering.

Theo's eyes tracked past it to the red barn beyond—picturesque, if you were into rustic postcards.

Then Nikos leaned forward, squinting. "What the hell is that?"

Theo followed his gaze—and nearly choked.

Parked beside the box truck was a van. Not just any van. A psychedelic, multicolored monstrosity—it looked as if the cast of Scooby-Doo had dropped acid and gone wild with a paint roller.

Nikos tilted his head. "Do you think they sell drugs along with their furniture?"

Theo didn't laugh. He couldn't even if he wanted to. His brain was too busy short-circuiting at the sight of the woman stepping out of said van.

*Rose.*

Her name whispered through his mind even as she turned at the sound of their tires against the gravel. Their eyes met. For a brief, hopeful moment, he thought maybe—just maybe…

But, no. He grimaced at the scowl of displeasure on her face. She shifted her weight, one hip cocked, arms folding slowly across her chest. Her chin lifted, her expression pure disdain—daring him to try her.

Nikos gave a low whistle. "Well… time and distance clearly didn't make her heart grow fonder."

Theo shot him a glare. "Stay in the car."

"Not a chance. I've got to have a peek inside the Mystery Machine. Maybe it has a minibar," Nikos murmured with a grin, already unbuckling his seatbelt.

"You're no help," Theo growled.

Nikos shot him a look of disgust. "No help! I'll remind you that I had to agree to a blind date to get us here. I think that is a tremendous sacrifice on my part. I've heard my share of horror stories about them."

"You might enjoy it," he defended.

Nikos shot him a pained expression. "She does walking ghost tours of New York, Theo—during the daytime. Do you really think she's going to be my type?"

"Probably not," he agreed, shooting Nikos an apologetic glance before he slid out of the SUV.

He stared at Rose in silence, afraid she might disappear. His gaze ran over the van when she turned to place a box inside.

*If she does run, and she does it in that van, at least it will be a hell of a lot easier to find her—even from outer space,* he mused.

He released a deep sigh and walked toward her. Once he was a couple of feet away, he stopped.

"Rose."

She arched one eyebrow and spoke in a voice sweet as vinegar. "Theo."

His gaze ran over the ridiculous van again. "That's an interesting vehicle."

"Thank you. I like it," she said.

He frowned, his gaze sweeping over her face. "You bought this... thing?" he asked, waving his hand at it.

She glanced over her shoulder at the van as if it was a beloved pet. "I did. Isn't she beautiful?"

"Beautiful?" He stared at her like she'd just announced she'd joined a traveling circus. "It looks like it was painted by a kindergarten class high on drugs."

"I said it looked like the Mystery Machine," Nikos piped up. "Hi, Rose."

"Nikos. Still shopping for friends under a rock, I see," she said with a fake smile before the smile faded and she looked back at him. "She has character, and she's mine—bought and paid for. No one can write a check and leave me *homeless* again."

"It's not what you think," he muttered.

"Oh? Did I misunderstand when you said you were going to call Mimi and quote 'tell her if the theatre wants a charitable donation, she'll have to terminate Rose's living and working arrangements. Immediately.' Or, what else did you say, Theo? That it was inevitable? You're right—it is. It was inevitable that I would be leaving you when I found out what a toad you are."

"I can explain," he growled in frustration.

Rose's eyes flicked to Nikos when he muttered, "I can't wait to hear this train wreck."

"Go take a walk, Nikos," she snapped at the same time as Theo scowled at his friend and said, "You're not helping!"

Nikos raised his hands and stepped toward the van. "I'll just go check out Rose's new home."

Theo muttered another curse and ran both hands through his hair. "I can't believe you gave up the chance to stay with me for—for that thing."

Her eyes glittered. "That *thing* is better than trading my life for billionaire bullshit."

Theo's jaw tightened. "Billionaire...? You left without giving me a chance to—"

"What? Explain? Manipulate me some more?" She took a deliberate step back, as if his very presence was something toxic. "No thanks. I've moved on. Greener pastures. Less... Greek tycoon drama."

"Greener pastures?" He took a step forward. "What does that mean? With whom?"

As if summoned by the universe to answer the question, a tall, broad-shouldered man with shaggy brown hair appeared from the house carrying a box. Robby Evans. Theo recognized him from the blurry traffic cam photo.

Robby strolled over, his dark brown eyes cool, and without breaking stride, slipped the box under one beefy arm while wrapping the other around Rose's shoulders where he pulled her close. It was casual, but the message in his glare was as subtle as a neon sign: *She's mine.*

Theo's pulse ticked up several notches.

"Who's your friend?" Robby asked.

Rose's lips pursed. "Just someone who took a wrong turn. He's leaving."

Nikos whistled and muttered under his breath, "This is gonna be good."

Theo ignored him—and Robby. His focus was on Rose. "We're not done."

She tilted her head. "We are now."

"You're on private property, Kallistratos. You might want to take your SUV and head back to whatever marble palace you crawled out of. Rose doesn't want you here," Robby said, nodding his head towards the driveway.

Theo's lips curved—not in humor, but in the smile that made grown men reconsider their life choices. "I didn't come this far to turn around."

Rose's scowl deepened. "Then be prepared to be disappointed," she snapped, twisting and walking away.

Theo balled his fists as Nikos stared with wide, amused eyes. Robby offered a nod filled with smugness. A soft curse escaped Theo as the broad-shouldered man put the box of treats he'd carried out into the van, then rushed after Rose.

She looked at him like he was poison. For a heartbeat, he believed it—before his pride smothered the doubt.

"Well, that went worse than I expected. What's next—kidnapping? Murdering the furniture guy?" Nikos asked, coming to stand beside him.

A sharp, predatory smile curved Theo's lips. He'd buy the entire damn farm if he had to—but he wouldn't need to. His Rose had thorns... and he'd bleed gladly to reach her.

"She'll run again," he said with confidence.

Nikos frowned. "Okay—and when she does?"

Theo flashed him a smile. "The van has two seats. I plan on being in one of them."

# Thirteen

From the upstairs bedroom window, Rose watched as Theo and Nikos made their way toward their SUV. Even from this distance, the stiff line of Theo's shoulders was unmistakable.

She rubbed her palms against her thighs, restless. She hadn't known Theo long, but she knew that jaw, that relentless focus—the way he decided something and then moved the world to make it happen. He'd been tenacious when he'd found her in New York, and he'd done it again here.

She didn't know how he'd tracked her down—it had to be through Kerry somehow—but she knew one thing for certain: he wouldn't give up easily.

The best way to keep a distance between them was to stay one step ahead. Which meant leaving. Tonight.

Her gaze lingered on the SUV longer than she intended. Theo opened the passenger door, but before getting in, he paused, his head turning slightly toward the farmhouse.

Her breath caught. Was he looking for her? Could he see her?

She stepped back from the window before she could find out, pressing her back to the wall. She had to move. Now.

She turned and began gathering the few things she'd unpacked, her movements brisk, efficient. Backpack first. Then the carry-on.

*Keep moving. Keep breathing.*

A quiet knock pulled her up short.

Robby leaned casually against the doorframe, his arms folded, his broad frame filling the space. But it was the look in his eyes—steady, possessive, tinged with something more—that made her chest tighten.

And just like that, she had another reason to leave tonight. Staying, even for one more night, would only complicate things—for both of them.

"You don't have to run," he said quietly. "I'll keep you safe."

A short, choked laugh escaped her, more brittle than she meant it to be. She shook her head. "I don't need to be kept safe, Robby. If anything, Theo's the one who needs a bodyguard."

His eyebrows drew together, but she pressed on before he could answer. "I really do appreciate everything you've done for me. More than I can say. But I... I need time to figure out who I am. Where I fit. And I can't do that if I'm..." She gestured vaguely toward him, toward the house, toward everything warm and solid about him. "... comfortable. I need to do this on my own."

"Why can't you do that here?" he asked, his voice quiet but weighted.

She met his eyes for a long moment. "I think you already know why."

Something shifted in his expression—acceptance, maybe, mixed with disappointment. He straightened from the doorframe and crossed the room toward her. She tensed instinctively but didn't pull away when he wrapped his arms around her.

"Kiss me goodbye, then?" he murmured.

She smiled sadly and nodded.

His kiss was warm, gentle, and comforting. But there was no spark. No breath-stealing rush. Not his fault—hers. Because deep down, she already belonged to a man she couldn't forgive.

When she broke the kiss, she left her hand on his chest for a beat, her gaze lowered. She wished she could feel something—anything—but all she felt was the absence of Theo.

"Worth a try," he said lightly, though she caught the flicker of something unguarded in his voice. "And if you ever think you'd like to try again, I'd be happy to volunteer."

She gave a watery laugh and sniffed. "I'll keep that in mind."

He stepped back, slipping easily into a lighter tone. "Dad and I will give the van a once-over before you head out. Mom's putting together a supply basket for you."

Her protest was immediate. "Robby, you don't have to—"

"Don't ruin her fun," he cut in with a grin. "There's fifty years' worth of stuff in this house, and Dad's been dying for an excuse to get rid of half of it. Consider it our contribution to your 'find yourself' adventure."

Her throat tightened again, this time from gratitude instead of grief. "Okay," she whispered.

She smiled, small but real, as he grabbed her backpack and carry-on. Together, they headed down the stairs. But as she reached the bottom, she glanced out the side window toward the long drive.

The SUV was gone.

Still, she had the uneasy feeling that Theo wasn't finished with her—not by a long shot.

By the time the neon glow of Sioux Falls' city lights shimmered ahead of her, Rose had driven through the night and half the morning, sustained by strong coffee, a few catnaps at rest stops, and the stubborn determination to put as much distance between herself and Theo Kallistratos as possible.

The atlas Belinda had insisted she bring lay in the passenger seat, its dog-eared pages soft from her study breaks. "You never know when your phone will lose signal," Belinda had warned in that matter-of-fact Midwest mom voice. "Paper doesn't glitch."

She'd plotted a loose loop in bright pink highlighter: Badlands National Park, then up into Montana to see Glacier National Park. Maybe even dip into Idaho and Wyoming, then meander back east through Colorado. National forests, state campgrounds, stretches of BLM land. She'd never left New York before—never had the time, the money, or the freedom. Now she had all three.

Somewhere, somehow, she'd find the place that felt like hers. Until then, she'd just... see everything.

She pulled into the grocery store lot with a mental checklist: bread, fruit, peanut butter, a few quick and easy meals she could prepare on the camp stove that came with the van, and maybe some cookies because adventure required cookies.

Her mood was lighter than it had been in days—until she rounded the corner of her van and jerked to a stop.

Theo was leaning against the passenger door like he'd been poured there, all dark suit and unreadable eyes.

Her disbelief lasted all of two seconds before it melted into flat-out exasperation. She didn't even speak. Just unlocked the side door and pushed the grocery cart closer.

A couple of teenagers in a beat-up sedan cruised past, whistling out the window. "Love the van!" one yelled.

Heat climbed her neck. She grabbed two bags and climbed inside, setting them on the narrow counter space. When she turned around, Theo was holding another bag out to her as if this was perfectly normal.

They worked in silence, passing bags, arranging groceries. She shoved the cold items into the van's tiny refrigerator, ignoring the way his presence seemed to take up more space than the van had.

By the time she shut the fridge, he was gone—returning the cart. She shut the side door and exhaled, but the relief was short-lived.

The passenger door clicked open.

Theo slid into the seat without a word.

Her eyebrows lifted. She said nothing, just walked around to the driver's side, got in, and started the engine. If he wanted a ride, fine. But she wasn't about to make this comfortable for him.

The first few minutes were quiet—if you ignored the squeal at a stop sign, the yellow-that-was-red, and the two near-collisions with locals who clearly didn't appreciate her 'creative' lane choices.

She could feel him watching her, his hand clamped on the grab handle above the door, the other gripping the seat so tightly his knuckles were bone-white.

Finally, through clenched teeth, he asked, "Exactly how long have you had your driver's license?"

She flashed him a bright smile. "Since I was sixteen."

His eyes narrowed. "And how long have you actually been driving?"

Her smile widened. "Counting yesterday? Two days."

If possible, his face went paler—with just a hint of green. "Perhaps," he said in a carefully controlled voice, "it might be best if I took over from here."

She made a show of thinking about it. "Hmm. Okay."

At the next service station, she pulled over, put the van in park, and smiled sweetly. "Would you mind getting me a bottle of cold water? Oh, and you can pay for the gas while you're at it—please."

He gave her a look but got out. She started the pump, filled the tank, and as soon as the nozzle clicked, she hopped into the driver's seat.

By the time Theo emerged from the store, water bottle in hand, she was already easing toward the road with the smug satisfaction of a woman making an exit. His look—half disbelief, half 'did you just dump my ass?'—was worth every mile of him grinding his teeth and stomping an imaginary brake.

*That's how you teach an arrogant jerk a lesson for getting into your vehicle without asking.*

The best part? The tiny thrill in her chest at the thought that he would absolutely come after her.

Her lips twitched. Then laughter burst out—hard, full-bodied, and bubbling—until she was giddy. The kind of laughter that made her forget, at least for a few minutes, why she'd been running at all.

If he hadn't been hanging on to the seat so tightly, Theo was fairly certain he would've slid right onto the floor of that ridiculous van at least twice during the drive.

Now, he was standing in the middle of God-knows-where, holding two bottles of water and a cup of coffee that looked and smelled like it had been brewed over a wood-burning stove.

One sip of burnt bitterness and the whole cup went straight into the trash.

He was contemplating his next move when his phone buzzed. When he saw the caller ID, he chuckled.

"Nikos," he greeted, lifting the phone to his ear. "Let me guess—you're calling to ask if I need a lift?"

"How did you know?" came the amused reply—just as a familiar SUV rolled into the next lane and stopped at the gas pump.

Theo arched an eyebrow and walked over. He opened the passenger door as Nikos slid out.

"Be a friend and grab me a coffee while I fill up," Nikos requested casually.

"No," Theo replied flatly. "I've already done that once today and got left behind for my trouble. Besides, the coffee here is undrinkable." He shut the door a little harder than necessary.

Nikos laughter rang out. *If Nikos isn't careful, he might just end up being the one stranded,* Theo thought, before he leaned his head back against the headrest. Nikos leaned against the open window on the driver's side, waiting for the pump to stop.

"How did you even know I needed rescuing?" Theo asked, buckling in.

Nikos chuckled again, looking far too pleased with himself. "Look in your coat pocket," he said, nodding toward it. "I put an Air tag in it. I put one in Rose's van, as well—just in case."

Theo turned slowly, his lips twitching despite himself. "She's going to kill you."

"Probably. I figured it might be a good idea to tag along for a bit. You know, make sure everything was… cool… before I headed back to New York." Nikos's grin widened. "When I got an alert that one air tag was moving and the other one wasn't, I figured you were in trouble. It took longer than I expected."

Theo snorted. "Trouble is a polite word for it."

"So… what exactly did you do this time?" Nikos asked, smirking.

Theo chuckled under his breath. "I might have… mentioned something about her driving."

There was a beat of silence—then Nikos burst out laughing, loud and unrestrained. "Oh, that explains it! You insulted a woman who just bought a psychedelic van. Of course she left you at a gas station!"

Theo laughed, deep and genuine, shaking off the last of his irritation. "She's going to pay for that," he said, his tone both fond and determined.

"Sure she is," Nikos replied, still grinning. "Just as soon as you catch her—for what is this—oh yeah, the third time."

Theo tore a candy bar in half and handed one piece over. "If we find a decent restaurant, stop. I'd kill for a proper cup of coffee."

Nikos took the candy, still chuckling. "Coffee, huh? You might need something stronger by the time this is all over."

Theo's smile widened. "The only thing I need… is Rose."

"So, is this what love feels like?" Nikos asked.

Theo looked out the window, warmth spreading through him. "Yeah," he said softly. "This is love."

# Fourteen

The rest area was nothing like she'd imagined when she pulled in. In her mind, 'rest area' meant ugly asphalt, buzzing overhead lights, and the occasional vending machine that may or may not eat your money.

This was… beautiful.

Her van sat at the far end of the winding loop that cut alongside a river, tucked under a cluster of old cottonwoods whose leaves whispered in the evening breeze. Close enough to the restrooms—elaborate outhouses, technically—but far enough from the main lot to feel private.

The bathrooms were surprisingly clean—almost enough to forgive them for being oversized porta-potties with wooden siding and a vent stack. A pump outside offered potable water, and there were picnic tables and grills scattered around, like the place had been designed with lingering in mind.

The air had shifted with sunset, turning crisp enough that she'd gone hunting for a blanket. Back in the city, summer nights clung to the heat. Here, the temperature dropped as if someone had flipped a switch.

She liked it. It felt… fresh.

Exhaustion had been stalking her since she'd left New York, heavier than the blanket draped around her shoulders. She and Robby had only slept in fits since leaving New York—three, maybe four hours sprawled in the back of the box truck—and she'd left before she'd even spent a single night in Omaha.

Now, soup simmered on her little propane stove. She set the pot on the picnic table, poured the soup into a tin camping mug that looked like it was from World War II, then carried it and her folding chair to the spot beside her van. Steam curled up, carrying the salty, familiar scent of chicken noodle.

She sipped slowly, letting the heat seep into her. The sky deepened from twilight to ink, the first stars pricking through. The more that appeared, the quieter everything seemed to grow—like even the breeze was leaning in to listen.

And then, inevitably, she thought of him.

Theo.

It wasn't fair, really. She'd put miles between them, yet the inside of her van still seemed to carry a trace of his aftershave—clean, sharp, warm in a way that tugged at her. She pulled the blanket tighter, tipping her head back toward the stars.

"Star light, star bright, first star I see tonight…" The old rhyme slipped out before she could stop it. The words were muscle memory, tangled with years of childhood wishes. "I wish…" Her throat tightened. "…I wish things could have worked out."

A breeze lifted a strand of hair across her cheek, and she brushed it back, annoyed at herself. *They might still…* The thought curled into her mind like a cat making itself comfortable.

Her frown returned as she replayed what Theo and Nikos had said— about her grandfather wanting confirmation that she *was* his granddaughter. She'd brushed it off, but now…

Her grandmother had always spoken like there was no place for Rose in that world. But grief made people say things. Losing Rose's mother would have been devastating. She remembered the haunted look in her grandparents' eyes whenever her father's name came up.

Maybe her mother's parents had changed their minds. Maybe they wanted to know her. And they were her only living family—at least, the only ones she knew about.

But even if she wanted to explore that, there was still the second issue.

Theo.

Her hand lowered to her stomach under the blanket almost without her realizing it. He'd said the condom had broken. Could she be pregnant? She hoped not—God, she hoped not—but if she was, she could make it work. She'd always made things work. A job, careful budgeting—those she could manage. She didn't need a man to raise a child.

What she didn't need—ever again—was manipulation. And Theo, for all his charm and all his intensity, had tried to control her. He should have told her what was going on, trusted her to make her own decision, instead of going full Greek-caveman.

Somewhere in the time since he'd shown up with no demands other than keeping her company, she'd forgiven him—but forgiveness wasn't surrender. Moving forward would be on her terms, not his.

A smile touched her lips as she remembered the dumbfounded look on his face when he first laid eyes on her van. Then she outright giggled, the sound bubbling up from her chest as she pictured his stranded figure at the gas station, his face a mask of disbelief as she drove away.

She shook her head, tilted her face back to the stars, and made her wish again. Deep down, she knew it would come true. Somehow, some way, it had to.

"Don't let him give up," she whispered.

She finished her last spoonful of warm soup as the stars densely populated the dark sky. She carefully packed her small stove, neatly folded the chair, and secured everything in the van. Once inside, she rinsed her mug, brushed her teeth, and pulled out the bed. The van creaked as she settled in, the thick quilt Belinda had insisted she take because it matched the character of her van, wrapping her in warmth against the night chill.

A soft sigh escaped her as she imagined it was Theo's arms. She'd only had one night, but she missed the feel of his body against hers.

She fluffed the pillow, sighed, and decided to review the map for tomorrow's journey. She was running her finger along the line of a highway when a light tap on the window jolted her. Her eyes flew to the window—and then she dissolved into laughter as she remembered her last wish.

She'd been found.

Again.

∼

"There's the van. You know, I thought she was crazy for buying something so... loud, at first, but now I'm glad," Theo said.

He had spotted the van immediately. Not that it was difficult—it looked like a kaleidoscope had crashed into a flower shop. The thing was parked under a cluster of trees, facing away from the main lot, as if that would somehow make it inconspicuous.

Nikos chuckled. "There's no way to miss it, that's for sure."

His mouth curved despite himself. His Rose was brilliant at hiding in plain sight.

"Now that we've found her again, what's the plan?" Nikos asked.

Theo grinned. "You drop me off and—" Nikos's snort of laughter cut him off, and he glared. "You think it's funny, but she'll have to take pity on me," he finished.

"Like she did at the gas station?" Nikos scoffed.

"This is different," he muttered.

"Hey, if you want to freeze your balls off and sleep on the ground, more power to you. We've been there, done that, once too often when we were in the military. I like my creature comforts now," Nikos stated in a dry tone.

"Well, the nearest creature comforts are forty miles away, and I'm not letting her out of my sight again," he muttered.

He switched the SUV headlights to the running lights as he pulled into the far end of the rest area.

The place was quiet, lit only by the soft glow from a couple of low, shielded lights in front of the bathroom. Rose's van was the only vehicle here.

The rest area was a lot nicer than some places he, Nikos, and the others had camped in during their military service. It was also a far cry from the penthouse skyline of New York. The fact that he and Rose weren't there—or in London, Paris, Athens, or Rome—was solely on his broad shoulders.

He shifted the SUV into park and unbuckled his seatbelt. He looked at Nikos when his friend grabbed his arm as he opened the driver's door.

"Are you sure about this?" Nikos asked.

Theo wasn't sure about anything. Normally, that would have concerned him.

*Well, normally that wouldn't happen, I would know what I was doing,* he mused with a rueful shake of his head.

"Give me ten minutes. If—if she doesn't let me in, then we'll go to Plan B," he muttered.

"Aren't we on Plan X, Y, or Z yet?" Nikos asked with a frown.

Theo huffed out a breath, grimacing at the visible puff in the cold air.

"Ten minutes," he groused, reaching for his thick, wool jacket in the backseat before he turned away.

He shoved his hands into the pockets of his jacket, thankful that he had it. His mind was running through all the ways Rose might react to his turning up again. Most of them left him feeling less than optimistic.

He slowed, breathing deeply as he approached the dark van. The thought that he might scare her occurred to him. He didn't want that.

There she was, curled inside, her face lit faintly by the warm glow of a small reading lamp, blanket to her chin, eyes heavy-lidded, and that stubborn crease still between her brows as she studied a large map.

For a moment, he just stood there. The instinct to tap the glass was strong, but so was the urge to watch her like this—at peace, or as close to it as she allowed herself.

Three days of chasing her had left him with too much time to think— about what he'd done wrong, how she'd left without hearing him out, and how he wanted her back for reasons beyond DNA or family ties.

He shivered as a brisk breeze wound through the canyon. He didn't do passive waiting—or dwell on the past—not when there was only a thin piece of glass and metal separating him from what he wanted.

He stepped forward and tapped the glass lightly with two fingers.

Her eyes flew to the window and widened with surprise. Then… she laughed. Not the brittle, defensive kind she'd given him before. Genuine laughter. The sound hit him square in the chest.

She scooted up, shaking her head at him like he'd just walked into a room wearing the wrong tuxedo. He could almost hear her: *Unbelievable. This man again.*

Theo fought to keep his own grin in check, but his lips betrayed him.

If she thought she could keep running, she was welcome to try. He had time. And patience. And a determination that had carried him through negotiations with billionaires twice as stubborn as she was—well, almost as stubborn.

The only difference was—he'd never wanted to win a deal as much as he wanted to win her.

Her giggles were still bubbling when she pushed the blanket aside and slid off the bed, shuffling to the side door.

She cracked it open just enough to peek out.

"You know, there's a word for men who keep showing up everywhere."

"Persistent?"

"Stalker."

"Mm." He tilted his head, the lamplight catching the faint curve of his smile. "That only fits if the subject of my attention isn't secretly pleased to see me."

She rolled her eyes, but the corner of her mouth twitched. "You have an over-inflated sense of your own charm."

"And you," he countered, "are terrible at hiding your smile when you're trying to be annoyed."

"Maybe I'm laughing at the irony—a billionaire in a bespoke suit lurking outside a flower-painted van. Not exactly your natural habitat," she shot back.

His gaze slid over the van with mock consideration. "I could learn to adapt."

"Not in those shoes you couldn't." She pushed the door open wider and leaned against the frame. "What are you doing here, Theo?"

"Catching up to you." Like it was the simplest, most inevitable thing in the world. "You ran off without hearing me out."

She crossed her arms, chilled, before she turned and pulled the blanket around her shoulders.

"You had your chance. You used it to talk about 'terminating my living and working arrangements'."

"That's not what I—" He cut himself off, exhaled slowly, and tried again. "I should have explained everything that night. I didn't. That's on me. But I'm here now."

She narrowed her eyes. "And you think showing up in the middle of the night at a rest stop is going to... what? Win me over?"

"I'm hoping you'll get so sick of me turning up, that you'll finally just accept that I'm not going to *give up*. You mean too much to me."

"What do you mean 'I mean too much to you'?"

He took a step closer, lowering his voice just enough to make her pulse trip. "And I mean this—"

He closed the distance between them. Her eyes flashed when he slid his hands reverently along her jaw. He hesitated a heartbeat, giving her time to pull away.

She didn't.

Neither of them moved. The air between them was cool and crisp and smelled faintly of pine from the trees above.

"You drive me crazy," she mumbled.

The smile forming on his lips disappeared when she leaned into him. He swore every kiss with her was a fireworks factory going off.

He groaned and pulled her closer. The blanket slid off her shoulders and tumbled around her knees. A shiver of need pulsed through him. When she started to pull away, a low protest slipped from him.

"Don't— Rose, please—" he muttered, gazing into her eyes.

"Where's Nikos?" she asked, her voice husky from their kiss.

He shrugged. "If it's been over ten minutes, he's on his way to a hotel about forty miles from here."

She pushed back against him, and he released her with a sigh of regret. He grabbed the blanket and wrapped it around her shoulders when she shivered.

She stared at him in disbelief before she shook her head. "Ten minutes? What happens if I pack up and leave your butt here?"

He gave her a crooked grin. "It will be a very long, unpleasant night. I don't suppose the bathrooms have a heater in them, do they?"

Rose closed her eyes, shook her head, and chuckled. "No, they don't have heaters. Plus, they are glorified porta-potties. I don't think you want to sleep in there."

"No, I would rather sleep with you. Where it is warm—for the sake of survival," he murmured.

She glared at him. "I'm the one who should be thinking about survival!" With a huff, she pushed open the van door farther and motioned for him to climb in. "It's going to be a tight fit. The bed's not all that big, and with it pulled out, there isn't much room inside."

He wiggled his nose in distaste. "We'll make it work. Unless—"

She turned at the skepticism in his voice and gave him a reproving glare.

"No, I'm not going to a hotel. You have the choice of the floor, the front seat, or the picnic table if you don't like it," she stated.

"I choose the bed," he said, shrugging off his jacket.

"What are you doing?" her voice squeaked out when his hands moved to his belt.

His lips curved when he unfastened it. Her eyes followed the movement of his hands as he undid his trousers and pushed them down.

"Getting comfortable. Skin-to-skin is better for keeping warm," he said.

"How would you know?" she asked, her eyes following his fingers as he unbuttoned his shirt.

"Five years in the military," he said.

She jerked her gaze up to his. "You were in the military?"

His expression softened. "Yes, *agápi mou.*"

"Oh." She paused and frowned as if she were trying to visualize him wearing a military uniform. "Did you ever have to get naked with other guys? Awkward—but I guess if you were half-dead you wouldn't care."

"Uh, no. Fortunately, that was never necessary. Shall I help you remove your clothing?" he asked with an amused smile.

"I'm fine," she said with a scowl.

She scooted over on the narrow bed so he could slide in. He straightened the covers and climbed in beside her wearing nothing but his boxers. She slid down and rolled onto her side, turning her back to him.

"I'm only doing this to keep you from freezing," she muttered over her shoulder. "Don't think this makes everything better."

He adjusted the covers over them before he wrapped his arm around her waist, pulling her close. She stiffened at first before pressing her delightful little rear end against his engorged cock. He ground his teeth when she wiggled back against him. Heat surged, sweat beading despite the cool night, and it took everything in him to hold the line.

He had always had a very active sex-drive, and knowing the deliciousness of the woman in his arms was enough to scorch his control.

Deciding it was best to think of something else, he forced his body to relax. He was surprised that the mattress was actually pretty comfortable, and while his feet were pressed up against the back doors, he could stretch out.

"Theo," Rose murmured, her voice drowsy with sleep.

"Yes, my Rose?"

"How did you find me so fast?" she asked.

"You get to blame Nikos this time," he chuckled. "This one's on him, but I'll tell you tomorrow, just in case you do decide to kick me out."

# Fifteen

Theo stepped out of the restroom, drawing in a lungful of crisp morning air. The early sun cast long, golden shafts through the cottonwoods, their leaves shimmering above him. His breath puffed faintly in the cool air, but it wasn't just the smell of coffee that drew him back to the van.

Rose was sitting cross-legged on the picnic table bench, steam curling from the enamel mug in her hands. She looked up when she saw him and held out a second mug toward him.

"Coffee," she said simply.

He took it, fingers brushing hers. "*Efcharistó*," he murmured, savoring the warmth against his chilled hands before taking a cautious sip.

She tilted her head, studying him. "Everything okay?"

"Yes. Why?"

"You're looking at me funny."

His lips curved. "Just… surprised you didn't leave me again."

She shrugged, a little smirk tugging at her mouth. "Would it have made a difference?"

"No," he admitted, shaking his head. "I'd find you again. No matter how long it takes. Unless you don't..."

Her eyes sharpened. "Unless I don't what?"

He hesitated. The truth lodged somewhere in his throat, heavier than he expected. She unfolded her legs and stood. Stepping closer, her gaze locked on his.

"Unless I don't what?" she repeated, softer this time.

He held her gaze, every instinct screaming at him to keep the words to himself. But he couldn't. He shook his head in response.

For the first time in his life, uncertainty clawed at him. He'd faced billion-dollar deals and life-or-death missions with more confidence. But nothing mattered as much as her—and if she told him it was over, he had no idea what he'd do.

Her hand lifted toward his face, her fingertips almost brushing his cheek... then she dropped it and turned away. His chest tightened, bracing for her to end things between them right there.

Instead, she tucked her hair behind her ear and said casually, "Breakfast is ready."

Relief swept through him so fast his knees almost buckled. He nodded once, willing his voice to work. "Thank you."

They sat next to each other, their mugs steaming between them. A bowl of oatmeal sat in front of him, dotted with raisins and sliced banana.

He eyed the bowl, his lips twitching with self-deprecating amusement. "You know, this is quite a decadent breakfast for a billionaire."

She grinned. "Don't I know it. I splurged on the cinnamon."

He ate a spoonful, pretending to consider it seriously. "Better than the pre-made food at the service station yesterday. I won't even mention their coffee. That... was a crime against humanity."

Her laughter bubbled out, as warm as the coffee. "That's what you get for insulting my driving. Be careful about doing it to my cooking. If you thought my leaving you at the service station was bad, it could get much worse."

He chuckled and leaned back, picking up his coffee cup and savoring another sip. "This is actually good—better than anything I've had in days."

"High praise," she teased.

"The highest," he confirmed gravely.

They fell into easy chatter, talking about the morning chill, the way the van had creaked under them last night, and—though neither outright said it—the fact that they'd shared the narrow bed. She made a crack about how he took up at least seventy percent of the mattress; he countered with how her blanket-hogging could be classified as a hostile takeover.

When she finally asked how he and Nikos had found her so quickly, he told her about the trail of traffic camera photos, Nikos' ridiculous agreement to go on a blind date, and Kerry's pointed hospitality offer involving 'a pot of boiling water'.

Rose giggled, her eyes bright with amusement.

"And then there were the air tags Nikos hid on both of us. Without them, I'd still be choking down that sludge from the service station," he added with amusement.

Her eyes widened and then narrowed. "Clearly your friends are far too used to putting the digital version of a child's leash on you," she joked.

His rueful, aggrieved expression had her cracking up, and by the time he finished eating, her eyes were dancing and her shoulders had relaxed in a way that made him feel like—for the first time in days—they were both breathing easier.

The laughter between them faded into a comfortable quiet. The steam from their mugs curled upward and disappeared into the pale morning light as she refilled them. Theo set his coffee down, his gaze lingering on her face until her smile softened with curiosity.

"What?" she asked, tilting her head.

He exhaled slowly, bracing his forearm on the picnic table. "I owe you an apology, Rose. A real one. And I think… it's past time you heard the truth."

Her expression stilled, but she didn't look away.

He took a breath. "Months ago, I had a meeting with Lorenzo Alliata. Business, mostly, but also… personal. He told me he was looking for someone—his granddaughter. Livia's daughter. He didn't have a name, only fragments of where she might be. I agreed to help, but I had no idea it was you. Not until…" His lips curved faintly. "Not until I saw your birthmark."

She tried for a wry smile, but her eyes searched his. "And my locket? Why did you take it?"

He hesitated only a moment. "I meant to give it back before you woke. I wanted to show Nikos because it proved what I already suspected. I recognized the photos of Livia and your father from the one Lorenzo showed me…. I knew your mother when she was younger. It was wrong, and I'm sorry. It seems like I'm always screwing things up when it comes to you." He sighed and shook his head. "Lorenzo isn't just my friend; he's my godfather. When I realized you were Livia's daughter, it should have changed things. I had crossed an invisible line. But it didn't matter. I still wanted you—like I've never wanted anyone in my life. And I know Lorenzo and Sophia… they're old-school Sicilians." He sighed, glancing toward the river before continuing. "They are fiercely protective of their family. They wouldn't approve of my seduction of their granddaughter."

Her brow furrowed deeper. "That's not what my grandmother told me. She told me they wanted nothing to do with me after I was born."

His gaze softened, his voice low. "That's something only Lorenzo and Sophia can explain. I'm asking you to please give them a chance. They are good people. Your mother had a twin sister—Lucinda—and a younger brother, Raff. He's my age.

"I should have told you the truth as soon as I recognized who you were. Not because of Lorenzo, not because of your family—but because you deserved honesty from the man who claimed to care about you," he continued quietly. "You captivated me the moment I laid eyes on you. Completely. There was just... something about you. And then you kissed me, and I swear to God, it knocked me sideways. I've closed billion-dollar deals with more composure."

Her face turned a rosy color that had nothing to do with the chill in the air. She studied him with a gaze that was a mixture of longing and uncertainty before asking, "And calling Mimi?"

His mouth curved, but the smile didn't reach his eyes. "I was being selfish. I wanted you all to myself. I didn't want to travel overseas and leave you behind."

Her gaze didn't waver. "And the marriage?"

Something in his jaw flexed. "The condom broke," he said simply. "In my—overly zealous—rush to have you."

He twisted and clasped her hands as emotion surged through him. "There's a chance you might be pregnant. And if you are..." his eyes locked on hers, the words warm and certain, "I'd be thrilled, Rose. More than thrilled. I never thought I'd want children—not until I met you. The idea of a little girl with your laugh..."

She swallowed. "And if I'm not?"

A slow, deliberate smile curved his lips as he leaned in, his voice dropping to a husky murmur. "Then it gives me more time to learn how to do things right."

Her breath caught as he brushed his mouth over hers—light, reverent —pulling back just enough to see her flush.

Rose turned, her mind swirling with everything he had told her. She cradled her mug between her palms, letting the warmth seep into her fingers as she watched a pair of dragonflies skimming over the river's surface.

It would be so easy to imagine mornings like this—coffee, damp earth, Theo beside her. Permanent. Too easy. If she stepped into that picture, she'd never want to leave. What scared her the most was that she wasn't sure she could survive watching it shatter if things between them fell apart.

He was watching her now, those dark eyes studying her as if he could read every thought running through her head. It made her feel both seen and bare.

She set her mug down slowly and turned to eat her oatmeal. "You make it hard to keep my guard up," she murmured.

His mouth curved, but there was a question in his gaze. "Let me in. Give us a chance to see where this will go, Rose. That's all I ask."

Her chest tightened at the simplicity of it—because he said it like it was possible. The only thing keeping them apart was a choice she hadn't yet found the courage to make.

She dropped her gaze to her hands, turning the spoon in her oatmeal, telling herself she was just buying time. But the truth was... she was already leaning toward him.

He was the danger—and the shelter. And that contradiction terrified her most.

"There are things I want to see and do," she said, watching a small bird hop across the ground on the other side of the table, its head tilting as if hoping she'd toss it a crumb.

"Like what?" he asked, leaning forward, genuinely curious.

She took a long breath. "I want to see if things can work out between us."

"They will." His answer was instant, certain.

She scoffed, shaking her head with a wry smile. "You say that as if it's a done deal. But you and I both know things haven't exactly been smooth sailing."

He reached up and caressed her cheek with the back of his fingers, his touch so gentle it made her breath catch. "They haven't been so bad either."

She laughed softly, but her gaze searched his. "Theo, I want to take my time with this. I want to… really know you. Not the man who can crook his little finger and have a bouncer ask a woman to the VIP lounge in the club he owns. Not the billionaire who can buy his way into—or out of—anything. I want to know the man who makes me laugh, the man who would travel halfway across the country to chase a woman… because he wasn't ready to let me go."

His thumb lingered along her jaw. "Doesn't that tell you who he is—and what he's willing to do for her?"

She released a breath. "Three weeks. My road trip—exactly the way I planned it." She watched his eyebrows lift, then added, "If you want to know me, then travel with me. Live like I live. See the things I want to see. Talk to me, spend time with me. Do all the crazy stuff that I've dreamed of, but have never done. And by the end of it… we'll both know if this can work. Plus…" She let the sentence hang.

"Plus?"

"By then we'll know if I'm pregnant or not."

That earned her a long, unreadable look before his gaze drifted toward the van parked under the cottonwoods. His voice was carefully even, but there was an almost comical inflection in it when he asked, "Does this journey of yours include… us traveling and sleeping in *that* van?"

Rose's grin widened. She didn't even try to hide her amusement. "It absolutely does."

He glanced down at his rumpled suit and designer wool coat, then back at her with the air of a man mentally calculating the number of showers he could tolerate missing. "I might need a different wardrobe if that's the case."

She laughed outright. "We'll stop at a thrift store. I'll help you pick something—don't worry, I have an eye for style."

His smile tugged into something quieter, more serious. "And what happens when our journey is over?"

Her expression softened. She hesitated, the question hanging between them like mist over the river, before she reached up and caressed his cheek.

"I don't know... not yet. But I do know I want to reach out to my grandparents first. Talk to them. Get to know them before I see them face-to-face." Her throat tightened. "And I'm still... grieving Pop. I don't want to rush that."

He kissed her—slow, deep, sure—then rested his forehead against hers. "I understand." His voice dropped to a whisper meant only for her. "This will be one adventure I'll never forget. And I wouldn't miss it for all the money in the world. I have only one request."

"What?"

"Can I please drive?"

Her laugh bubbled out, joyous and free, as she leaned back. "Yes, you can drive, because our next stop is—" She launched into an excited explanation, her hands painting the route in the air.

And as she spoke, she felt her heart swell at the sight of him— rumpled, determined, and sitting in the chill morning air just to be near her. She realized then that Theo had never needed a sword to cut through the wall of thorns she'd built around her heart.

He'd only needed a tender caress—and the way his thumb brushed over her knuckles now proved it.

For the first time, the road ahead didn't feel like escape. It felt like the beginning of something she might finally call home.

# Sixteen

Three weeks and nearly five thousand miles later, Theo stretched out in the sable leather seat of his jet, feeling the hum of the engines' purr beneath him. It was a familiar sound, one that usually blended into the background of endless business flights. But today, his entire body seemed attuned to it—relaxed, satisfied, and humming with contentment.

Against all odds—and despite his very vocal reservations at the start—he'd driven Rose's kaleidoscope-on-wheels van across more than half the United States. Somewhere between the Badlands, Big Bend, and the long road back to New York, he'd discovered something unexpected: exhilaration.

They had laughed over terrible diner pie, marveled at what life must have been like for early indigenous people, and fallen asleep to the sound of wind rattling the van's pop-top. The last time he'd felt that free—this unbound—was when he and Alexandros had been teenagers, before life had come calling with its responsibilities, expectations, and inherited titles.

His gaze softened as he studied Rose. She was leaning toward the steward, discussing something with that bright, animated smile that still caught him off guard. The cabin light caught the glint of red in her hair and the warmth in her eyes, and for a moment, he just... let himself watch her.

Two weeks ago, they'd learned she wasn't pregnant. He'd been surprised by his own disappointment, and he'd sensed she felt the same. But as he'd told her—quietly, honestly—it gave him more time to get things right.

A soft ping drew his attention to his phone. A message from Nikos.

*Everything going alright?*

Theo smirked and tapped back: *More than alright. We're on our way to Athens.*

It surprised him to hear from his friend. Nikos had been distracted ever since his so-called 'blind' date a week ago, a detail Theo fully intended to press him about later.

Before he could pocket the phone, another message came in. This one from his father.

*Will you handle the meeting in Athens, or should I or Alexandros take care of it?*

Theo's jaw flexed. He'd been evasive with his family over the past month, deliberately so.

*I'll attend the meeting,* he typed back. Then, after a moment's hesitation: *And I'll be visiting Syros. I have someone I would like you and mother to meet.*

He left it at that. He would explain who Rose was in person. Rose had asked for the same caution—she didn't want her grandparents knowing about their relationship yet. Over the last three weeks, she'd spoken with them often via video calls. At first, she'd been nervous, hesitant. But now... now she seemed almost eager to meet them.

He looked up to find her studying him.

"Everything alright?" he asked.

She nodded and smiled. "Yes, everything's good. It feels strange not being in the van."

He chuckled. "It's not much different," he teased. "I wanted to let you know—we'll be going to my family's home on Syros. I would like to introduce you to them. I'll need to fly to Athens during the day for meetings, but I'll be home each evening."

Her brow furrowed slightly. "Wouldn't it be easier to stay in Athens until your meetings are over?"

"It would," he admitted, a small smile tugging at his mouth. "But I thought you'd be more comfortable at the villa on the island."

She considered that, then smiled faintly. "Maybe after you're finished. But... I'd really like to see Athens first."

He chuckled and inclined his head. "Athens it is."

They hadn't talked about it yet, but his plan was already set. Whether in Athens or Syros, it didn't matter.

*Soon,* he promised himself.

Dinner was as flawless as it was intimate, a quiet cocoon of good food, low conversation, and glances that lingered longer than they should have. By the time they retired to rest, Theo's mind was no longer on meetings, villas, or even the long miles behind them.

It was on the moment, in just a few days' time, when he would ask her the only question that mattered.

Three days in Athens and she was already running on fumes.

Her days were spent roaming the city—temples, markets, museums— while Theo was locked in back-to-back meetings. Then, as soon as evening hit, it was one social event after another. Charity galas, gallery openings, and cocktail hours with people whose teeth were suspiciously perfect and whose smiles didn't reach their eyes.

By the time they staggered back to his apartment each night, she was exhausted. She didn't know how Theo kept up. Work all day, socialize half the night, fend off the paparazzi—who buzzed around them like over-caffeinated mosquitoes—and still wake up looking like he'd stepped out of a GQ spread.

She was ready to crawl back into her van; quiet mornings of oatmeal, questionable coffee, and long aimless drives sounded like paradise. She missed the way they'd fallen asleep to the sound of the wind and woken to sun spilling across the dashboard and birds singing at an ungodly hour.

She'd bailed on the scheduled event for the evening, pleading fatigue. As she returned to the apartment in the late afternoon, she was glad.

She keyed in the door code, stepped inside—

—and froze.

Her frown deepened at the trail—scarf on the couch, blood-red stilettos abandoned mid-hallway. She stopped dead in the bedroom doorway.

The bed was a tangle of rumpled sheets. On the floor, pooled like discarded skin, lay a matching blood-red designer dress, a black thong, and a lacy bra that had never seen the inside of a discount store.

A splash of water from the bathroom pulled her forward.

Rose nudged the door open with the toe of her tennis shoe.

The woman in the tub tilted her blond head back and smiled like she'd been expecting champagne— and company. One perfectly tanned leg lifted out of the water, showing off crimson-painted toenails.

"Hi, Theo. Welcome home, darling," the woman purred.

Rose leaned her shoulder against the doorframe, crossed her arms, and raised one eyebrow.

The woman twisted toward her, flashing a sweet, fake smile.

"Theo's not here, I am. And you are…?" Rose asked.

"Gina," the woman replied, with the kind of confidence that implied the name should mean something. "I'm a very *good* friend of Theo's."

Rose's lips curved, but there was nothing warm in it. "You have exactly five minutes to get out of the apartment before I call security... Gina."

Gina rose, unconcerned with her nakedness, water sliding over skin maintained with more money than Rose's van had cost. "And who are you?"

Rose checked an imaginary watch. "Four minutes, thirty seconds."

Rose knew her voice was cool, her smile sharp—but her hands still shook faintly as she texted Theo. Not from fear. From fury. From the knowledge that once again, someone was trying to wedge themselves between her and the one man she wasn't ready to lose.

*Do you know why there's a naked woman named Gina taking a bath in our bathroom?*

Her phone pinged almost immediately, this time with an incoming call.

Rose smiled sweetly and answered. "Hi, Theo."

She turned on her heel, walking through the bedroom, down the hallway, and into the living room.

Theo's voice came through tight with fury. "Gina is a friend of the family—but not, and I repeat *not*, that kind of friend."

Rose's gaze flicked to a damp, pouting Gina stomping into the room dressed only in lace. "Then someone should probably tell her that."

"I will. Put her on the phone."

Rose handed the phone over, keeping her expression neutral.

She heard Theo's voice even from a few feet away—cold, controlled, and dangerous in a way that made Gina's complexion go pale. The woman sniffed once, inelegantly, and returned the phone without a word.

"Security's on their way up," Theo said. "I don't know who gave her a key, but I promise you—this will never happen again."

A knock sounded at the door just as Gina pulled the sleeve of her unzipped dress over her shoulder.

"Hold on. I think they're here," she said, walking forward to answer the door. "Hey, guys. Thanks for coming so quickly to take the trash out."

"Bitch," Gina hissed under her breath as she stomped past, carrying her killer stiletto heels by the straps in one hand.

"That's *Ms.* Bitch to you. And in case you didn't get the message... I'm more than a *friend* of Theo's," Rose said, smiling sweetly and winking at the two security guards who were doing their best to keep a straight face.

Gina shot one last glare over her shoulder, lifted her chin, and stalked out past the two security officers.

Rose set the phone to her ear again.

Theo was still apologizing.

"You can finish apologizing when you get home," she said. "Right now I need to bleach the bathroom and change the sheets, because I am not bathing or sleeping in either until they've been sanitized."

"I'll have housekeeping take care of it," Theo said instantly. "Why don't you come to my office? We'll go out for dinner. Somewhere cozy, romantic, just the two of us."

"Not dressy?" she asked hopefully.

He laughed. "Not dressy. I know the perfect place. A driver will pick you up in twenty minutes."

"Thank you," she replied.

She hung up and walked to the window.

Athens sprawled beneath her in a breathtaking patchwork of light and shadow, ancient and modern colliding at every turn.

For a moment, she let herself imagine the quiet life she'd left behind—the one without strangers in bathtubs or cameras flashing in her face.

But then she remembered how empty it had been before Theo.

There was no way she was ready to give that up.

~

Theo's jaw tightened as he ended the call from security confirming Gina Rossi had been escorted out of his building.

He could still feel a low burn of anger in his chest.

Immature. Impulsive. Self-centered. Gina had always been all of those things. But this—breaking into his private residence and pulling a stunt like this—was something else entirely.

It wasn't just the invasion of his space. She had tried to damage what he had with Rose. And that… that was unforgivable.

His phone lit up with Gina's name.

For a moment, his thumb hovered over the Decline button. But no—he wanted her to know she'd crossed a line that could never be uncrossed.

"What do you want, Gina?" His voice was flat, controlled.

Her tone was breathless, almost childlike. "Please, Theo, don't tell my father. I wasn't thinking—"

"That much is clear."

"I just—" She faltered, then blurted, "I saw the photos of you and her in the tabloids. I was jealous. I thought…"

"You thought wrong." His voice cut like glass. "And don't bother reminding me of some imaginary marriage arrangement between you and my brother. That never happened, and even if it had, it's irrelevant."

She tried to protest, but he'd had enough.

"If you don't stay away from me—and from Rose—your father knowing about your behavior will be the least of your worries. Am I clear?"

There was a small, sulky pause. "…Yes."

The moment he ended the call, his phone lit up again.

He groaned. Allegra Rossi.

For a second, he contemplated ignoring her too. But if Allegra was calling, it was because Gina had already run crying to her sister. He might as well deal with it now.

"Allegra," he said, keeping his tone polite but clipped. "What do you need?"

"Welcome home," she began carefully. "I... I just spoke to Gina. She told me what happened."

"Then I assume you also know I'm not in the mood for excuses."

"She was wrong," Allegra said quickly. "Both of us are mortified. Gina has always... had issues with rejection. I'm not asking you to forget it, Theo, but I am asking for understanding. She needs help, and—"

"What she needs is to stay away from me and Rose," he said sharply. "And if she does that, I won't discuss this with your parents."

There was a brief silence before Allegra's voice softened. "Are things serious between you and... this Rose?"

"Yes," he said simply. "Very serious."

Another pause, then Allegra exhaled. "Then I wish you happiness. I'll speak to Gina."

"Thank you." He ended the call before she could say more.

He sat back, muttering under his breath about manipulative, spoiled individuals, and silently prayed Vito wasn't next on the list.

A knock at the door interrupted the thought.

His PA stepped in, holding the door open. "Ms. Smythe to see you, sir."

Theo rose to his feet, his eyes glued to Rose.

All thoughts of Gina, Allegra, and the day's aggravations dissolved like mist under the sun. He pushed away from his desk and crossed the room in three long strides, opening his arms.

Her smile—the real one, not the polite mask she wore at social events —struck him square in the chest.

He drew her in, breathed her in, the feel of her petite frame against him resetting his world. "Ready for dinner?"

"Depends," she said with a little curve of her mouth. "Where are we going?"

His lips tugged into a slow smile. "Someplace private. Romantic."

An hour later, she stood on the polished teak deck of the *Kallistratos Challenge*, the city lights of Athens glittering on the water behind her. The sea air teased her hair, and the yacht's low thrum was the only sound besides the faint lap of waves.

Theo swore he'd never seen a more beautiful woman in the world as he gazed across at Rose. The candlelight flickered, caressing her face and making her eyes shine as they lingered over a dinner under the open sky. It didn't matter how much time they spent together, there was always something to talk about.

He stood and held out his hand to her. Her smile softened, and she walked with him over to the railing where they stood looking out across the glittering metropolis of Athens. He pulled her close, loving how her body fit against his.

"You know, when I made those comments about you being a billionaire, I was only joking. I didn't know it was true," she said, relaxing into him with a sigh.

He chuckled. "I liked that you never cared about the 'billionaire bullshit'."

She laughed. "It has its perks."

"It does, but so did living in your van," he murmured, turning her around to face him. He framed her face in his hands. "This is where I want to be. With you. Always. I love you, Rose."

# Seventeen

Rose felt like she was floating on air as she stepped off the yacht beside Theo the next morning. The golden light of dawn reflected off the water in a shimmer that matched the glow in her chest. She bit her bottom lip, fighting the urge to grin like a loon, as she thought about the night before. Theo kept a firm grip on her hand as they walked together toward the waiting car.

Tomorrow, they'd travel to Syros, to his family's villa. But tomorrow was tomorrow.

She kissed him at the curb, quick and playful. "You're going to be late for work if you don't leave."

His eyes darkened, his mouth tilting into that wicked smile that always made her knees feel unsteady. "I'm the boss, *agápi mou*," he growled. "Who's going to fire me?"

Her breath caught at the expression in his eyes. She cupped his jaw, her thumb brushing the rough edge of his stubble. "I love you, Theo."

He answered with a kiss that devoured the words.

He lifted her against him, his arms locking her in place, and kissed her like he'd been starved for years. She clung to him, her heart pounding, until she was rosy-cheeked and breathless. Her eyes locked with his as she slid slowly down his body.

She became keenly aware of his driver and bodyguards, standing discreetly but close enough to see everything. Her cheeks burned hotter.

"I'll see you tonight," she said, stepping back, her voice soft and filled with warmth.

She waved as the car door closed behind him. Longing filled her as she watched until the taillights vanished into the morning traffic. With a sigh, she turned to her driver.

"Good morning, Christian. How would you feel about exploring Delphi today?"

Christian's weathered face broke into a smile. "A wonderful choice, Miss. It's about two and a half hours if the roads are clear. It's a beautiful drive."

"I call shotgun," she laughed, moving to the front passenger side.

"You always do," Christian chuckled.

Rose sank back in the plush seat of the Audi as they left the city behind, trading marble facades for rolling hills and distant mountains.

She loved chatting with Christian. He was a new grandfather, married to the love of his life after meeting her at a seaside café nearly forty years ago, and a wonderful tour guide as he knew the area so well.

She shared growing up in the theatre with him, telling him stories of her grandparents, the performers she had met, and the amazing plays she had been fortunate enough to see. It felt like that part of her life was an eternity ago.

An hour outside of Athens, the highway narrowed into winding ribbons of asphalt cutting through olive groves and rocky slopes.

Rose sat forward, watching sunlight flash through the trees as they rounded a sharp curve. Christian muttered something under his breath in Greek as she lifted her phone and snapped a photo of the road ahead of her, along with several more of the views to her right and a funny selfie to share with Kerry.

"What is it?" she asked.

"Holiday drivers," he said with mild irritation. "Everyone thinks they are a rally champion."

She grinned. "They must be from New York."

He chuckled, easing into the turn. "You have driven in New York?"

She shook her head with a mock expression of horror. "I've survived New York. Driving there? I'm not that brave."

Christian chuckled at her confession. "Sometimes I feel like that driving in Athens. I am beginning to think I will add this road to my list," he added when a dark sedan pulled abruptly in front of them, forcing him to slow.

"Yep. Looks like New Yorkers," she teased, noticing that another vehicle eased up on their bumper.

She snapped a few more photos before she sent them to Kerry with a *'Guess where I am now! Heading to explore Delphia. Drivers here are as bad as back home. Wish you were here. Miss you!'*

Her smile faded when the lead car veered onto a side road and they could now see that ahead, orange cones and a man in a reflective vest waved them toward the narrow turnoff.

"It looks like we may be taking the scenic route," Christian said with an apologetic smile.

"That's okay. It just means I get to see more of the countryside," she replied.

The road tightened, the cliff face rising on one side and the drop-off yawning on the other. Rose tried to ignore the knot forming in her stomach as she peered over the edge.

Christian was still talking about aggressive Greek drivers when they rounded another bend—

—and the sedan ahead of them was suddenly stopped dead in the middle of the lane.

"What the—" Christian slammed on the brakes.

Rose's seatbelt bit into her shoulder as the car jerked to a violent halt. Before she could process what was happening, two men spilled out of the sedan—both from the passenger side, moving fast, their faces shadowed under masks.

Her pulse spiked. "Christian—"

Two sharp pops shattered the morning calm. The Audi sagged in back —the tires blown.

"Rose, call Theo," Christian said in a low, urgent voice.

She fumbled for her phone—no time to scroll for his number. Her eyes flashed to the video icon, and she pressed it, hoping that Kerry wasn't at work or asleep and would answer it. The ping of Kerry answering was drowned out by the sound of shattering glass. Rose flinched as the driver's side window exploded inward, spraying shards.

"Hey, girlfriend. I just got your photos," Kerry said.

"Kerry... call Theo! Oh, God! Call Theo!" Rose cried out as Christian's body jerked violently.

"Rose, what's going on?!" Kerry demanded.

"Christian!" she screamed, fumbling with her phone as his hands spasmed on the steering wheel as a bright arc of electricity flashed through the broken window.

The acrid tang of ozone burned her nose—taser.

"Rose! Tell me what's happening!" Kerry urged with heightening alarm.

A hand shot in through the driver's side, slapping at the door controls. The locks clicked open.

"They're going to take me. Call Theo. Tell him—"

Her door was yanked wide before she could move.

"No! No! Let me go!" she cried out, twisting and shoving at the arm that reached for her.

"Tell him… I love him—"

If this was the last thing she ever said, let it be that. That she loved him. Fiercely. Without regret.

Her nails dug into the black fabric of her attacker's arm as she fought to break free. Her body jerked when she felt a sharp prick in her upper arm that stole her breath.

Cold fire tore through her veins, each heartbeat slower, heavier.

"No—" Her voice broke and slurred as her limbs went heavy. She clung to her phone as long as she could, trying to give Kerry as much information as she could before she lost consciousness.

"The… photos—"

Her fingers numbed until her phone slipped from her grasp and clattered between the seats.

Her vision swam. The men's voices were distant, muffled.

She tried to resist when she felt herself being lifted. Her head lolled against a solid chest. Outside the car, the world tilted, the sunlight flashing in and out of view through the swaying gap of an open car door.

The metallic slam of a door. The sickening thought that she might never see Theo again—

—then nothing.

The surrounding office was all polished glass and sharp edges, but Theo's mind wasn't on the merger projections scrolling across the digital display. It was on Rose.

On the way her eyes had softened this morning when she'd cupped his face and the way she'd whispered *I love you* before kissing him.

His fingers drifted to his pocket, closing around the small velvet box he'd been carrying for the past week. The ring had been burning a hole in his pocket since the day he bought it. He'd planned to wait until Syros—but last night, one kiss had nearly burned that plan away.

He'd wanted her so fiercely it had drowned out the words he should have said. And though he'd told her he loved her, she hadn't said it back. Not then.

*Tomorrow,* he told himself. *Tomorrow, when I won't be interrupted.*

The soft click of the door pulled him from his thoughts. Markos Aetos stepped in, his tall frame filling the doorway.

Theo rose, clasping his hand. "Markos. What brings you to Athens? I thought you were in Paris."

"I wanted to see how the new merger was progressing before heading over to New York for a few weeks," Markos said, taking a seat and stretching his legs out.

"Worried I wouldn't make it?" he joked.

Markos chuckled. "And I wanted to hear about the woman who captured the great Theo Kallistratos."

"Her name is Rose. She's amazing, Markos." He paused, lost in the vision of her last night. "I'm going to ask her to marry me."

"Marry! Wow, I wasn't expecting that. You've only known her for how long?" Markos asked, straightening in his chair to stare at him in shock.

"A little over a month," Theo confessed.

"Are you sure about this? Hell, Nikos told me she was Livia's daughter, but damn, from the look on your face, I'm assuming this isn't an arranged marriage. How did Lorenzo react?" Markos demanded.

"He doesn't know yet," he admitted.

"You love her," Markos said.

Theo smiled. "Yeah. I love her."

"More power to you, man."

Theo relaxed back as Markos asked him about the newly acquired surveillance tech firm he had been drooling over for the past year. The AI-facial recognition advancements alone would be a game changer not just for corporate security, but for high-level government contracts.

When there was a lull, Theo asked, "Have you talked to Nikos lately? I forgot to ask him how the London merger went."

Markos shook his head. "Not since London. He said it went well. He was heading back to New York while I headed to Paris."

Theo was about to ask how the Paris merger went when his phone rang. He grinned faintly at the caller ID.

"Speak of the devil—" He answered. "Nikos—"

The voice on the other end was clipped and urgent. "Theo. Kerry just called me. She's hysterical. She said Rose has been taken."

Theo's knees buckled, his chest constricting until he couldn't breathe. It felt like someone had ripped the ground from beneath him, leaving only a freefall into hell.

"What?! What are you talking about?"

"I'm heading to Kerry's apartment now," Nikos continued, his voice terse with tension. "I'll call you as soon as I know more."

Theo swayed, bracing hard against the desk, white-knuckled. "Keep me updated." He ended the call, his throat tight, and looked at Markos. "Nikos just told me... Rose—she's been kidnapped."

"Kidnapped?"

Theo was already moving, his phone in hand, dialing Rose. The call went straight to voicemail.

He tried Christian's number next.

Voicemail.

His pulse pounded in his ears. He hung up—and his phone pinged with a series of incoming messages. He glanced at the number.

*Kerry.*

A second later, it rang.

He answered on the first beat. "Kerry?"

Her voice was trembling, thick with tears. "Theo, I just found your number. Rose… sent me these. We were video chatting when… when it happened. I didn't know what to do—she—"

"Kerry. Tell me everything."

"She said… she said they were taking her. She told me to tell you she loves you." Kerry's voice broke. "She also said something about photos. These are the only ones I could think of—she just sent them before—before—"

Theo's grip tightened on the phone until the casing creaked. "Listen to me. Nikos is on his way to you. You need to remember everything Rose said. Everything you saw. We will get her back. I promise. We'll get her back."

He ended the call before his voice cracked.

For a moment, he simply sat, his body folding into the chair as if the air had been punched from his lungs. Theo swiped blindly, his hands shaking, barely seeing through the haze.

The picture on the screen was of Rose. She was making a goofy face, the sun flaring behind her over some scenic stretch of road.

He swiped to the next.

Markos's shadow fell across him. Without a word, the other man reached down and took the phone from his limp fingers, scrolling through the images.

Then he froze. "Theo… she's brilliant. Look—" He turned the screen. In the background of one shot, the bumper of a dark sedan filled half the frame, the license plate visible. In another, a blurred profile—a man's face, caught mid-turn.

Markos looked up, his expression grim. "She gave us their car. And maybe one of them."

Theo rose, his shock replaced with cold and razor-sharp determination. "Call in Angel and Cole," he said, his voice low and lethal. "Let's see how good that new software really is."

# Eighteen

Rose woke to the sound of shouting.

Not the distant, muffled kind from a neighbor's apartment. This was close—just outside the bedroom door.

Her lashes parted the tiniest fraction, letting in a slice of pale daylight. The room was... disarmingly normal—modern, clean, and even tasteful, with pale cream walls, a low-slung oak bed frame, matching nightstands, and a sleek dresser.

A wide window framed by gauzy white curtains let in soft, late afternoon light. The faint scent of dried flowers hung in the air, as if someone had actually tried to make this place pleasant.

No bars. No guards. No restraints.

That unsettled her more than chains would have.

She pushed up onto an elbow, pressing trembling fingers to the dull ache at her temple. The voices were muffled, but one—female, sharp— cut through clearly enough to make out the tone: furious.

A second later came a screech that could have stripped paint.

There was a distinct sound of scuffling as the female voice moved closer.

Rose let her body go slack, her breathing deepening into the slow, even rhythm of someone asleep. Stillness could be as much a performance as movement. She had learned that from different performers over the years and finally understood what they meant.

The door lock clicked. The hinges creaked.

A woman stumbled into the room, shoved forward by a man who— though not tall—had the kind of square, muscled frame that filled the doorway. His black windbreaker hung loose, but his forearms were thick and corded.

The woman spun toward him, snapping something in rapid-fire Italian. The man's answer was a vicious slap, sharp enough to echo.

Rose's gut tightened with fear.

The woman staggered, catching herself with one hand on the dresser near the door. Her glossy blonde hair fell across her face, barely hiding the raw bloom of his handprint.

The man barked a guttural threat in Greek—too low for Rose to catch —then turned his gaze toward the bed.

She let her lids lower again, her body sinking into the mattress, keeping her breathing steady.

A beat later, the door slammed, and the lock slid home.

The woman was instantly at the door, pounding with her fists, her voice rising in another furious stream of Italian.

Rose waited until the tirade ebbed, then opened her eyes fully.

The woman turned.

There was no fear there. Only pure, unfiltered fury.

"This is all your fault!" she snapped in accented English.

Rose pushed up slowly, frowning. "Sorry... what exactly is all my fault?"

"You ruined everything!" The woman flung her hands up, bracelets clinking. "If you hadn't wiggled your wares in front of Theo—if you'd just taken the hint after Gina went to the apartment—none of this would have been necessary! I wouldn't be in this mess!"

Rose blinked. She was locked in a badly written horror show. "I have no idea what you're talking about. What does Theo have to do with this? And how did you know about Gina being in the apartment?"

The woman's lip curled. "Theo Kallistratos should have been mine."

*Ah, that explained the fury, if not the rest of the crazy.*

Her runners sank into the thick cream rug beneath her. "And you are…?"

Up close, Rose took in more detail. The woman's clothes—expensive but rumpled—looked like they'd been slept in. Her mascara had smudged faintly, but her peppermint-pink nails were immaculate.

The woman ignored the question, turning away to rub her cheek where the red handprint was already swelling. Her movements were jerky, defensive—like someone who'd been knocked off-balance and wasn't used to it.

"Who are you?" Rose repeated, sharper this time, studying the woman like she might study a tiger.

Resentment flickered in the woman's eyes, but something else too—a quick flash of embarrassment, maybe even shame—before she dropped her chin. Her shoulders trembled.

And then she started to cry.

Rose stared for a long beat, then let out a slow sigh.

*Okay, emotional whiplash. But crying means she's rattled… rattled means she might talk.*

She stood, padded to the bathroom, and returned with a cold, damp washcloth. Wordlessly, she held it out.

The woman hesitated—pride stiffening her spine—before she took the damp cloth and pressed it to her cheek.

"Let's start over," Rose said, her voice gentler. "I'm Rose. And you are?"

The woman's reply was tight, almost bitten off. "Allegra Rossi."

"Rossi?" Rose repeated, the name clicking in her mind like a puzzle piece sliding into place. "Wait. You mentioned Gina a second ago. Are you related to Gina Rossi?"

"Yes. She's my half-sister."

Rose blinked in surprise. "Okay. I wasn't expecting that." She eased back onto the bed, partly to keep the room from tilting, partly to keep Allegra talking. "Do you know who took us?"

Allegra nodded sharply. "Yes."

Rose stayed quiet, letting the silence stretch just enough to make it uncomfortable. People filled silences—they couldn't help it.

Allegra finally spoke. "I did. Well... sort of. It was just a suggestion. I had no idea *he* would actually do it."

Rose's brows shot up. And there it is—the crazy twist. "...You hired them?"

Allegra's mouth flattened into a scowl. "I suggested it. I didn't do the actual hiring."

"You suggested it?" Rose gave a sharp laugh. "Great. My alternate universe theory that there's a sane one and a crazy one has official been confirmed," she grumbled with disbelief. "So—who did you sort of hire/suggest to kidnap me, and why?"

Allegra sighed, setting the washcloth on the bed. "My stepbrother, Vito, is the one who hired whatever misguided idiots he could find. He needed money, and I wanted Theo. It was a two-birds-with-one-stone type of transaction. I had no idea Vito would actually be stupid enough to do it," Allegra scoffed with a dismissive wave of her hand like there were no laws being broken.

"I'm guessing your family get-togethers are... interesting," Rose muttered, because really, what else could she say?

## Kallistratos Family Villa: Syros, Greece

Alexandros Kallistratos had just decided that paperwork could wait when Dani shifted on his lap, her mouth brushing his in a kiss that was far more interesting than quarterly projections.

Her laugh was soft against his lips when his phone buzzed somewhere behind her hip.

He groped blindly across his desk, still trying to keep the kiss going. "Ignore it," he muttered.

Dani slid off his lap with a teasing smile. "Break time's over."

He groaned. "Who decided that?"

"Your phone," she said, already walking toward the door.

He glanced at the caller ID and nearly groaned again. Vito Marino. Exactly the sort of person who could ruin a perfectly good day. He thumbed to answer, already planning the shortest possible conversation.

"What?" Alexandros said flatly.

What came back was… noise. A desperate tangle of words—half apologies, half incoherent rambling—that included Theo's name and a woman named Rose.

"Vito," Alexandros cut in. "Slow down. English, Italian, or Greek. Not all three. Words in order. Try again."

"I'm sorry," Vito blurted. "I'm sorry for everything I've ever done—okay, maybe not everything—but this one, this one's bad. Theo is going to kill me. I wouldn't blame him. But it wasn't supposed to turn out this way, you understand? I owe the wrong people money, and Allegra had this wonderful plan—you know, just a minor delay, nothing serious—"

Alexandros pinched the bridge of his nose. "Delay for what?"

"To give her time to... uh... seduce Theo."

That made him straighten. "What did you do, Vito?"

There was a beat of silence. Then—

"I might have helped... kidnap Theo's woman. Her name is Rose something. She's in the tabloids. Very photogenic."

"Are you admitting that you *kidnapped* Rose... Rose Smythe?" Alexandros's voice sharpened. "Lorenzo Alliata's granddaughter, Rose Smythe?"

On the other end, Vito released a low, miserable groan. "If Theo doesn't kill me, Lorenzo will. And if Theo and Lorenzo don't, my father will. And my mother. Possibly my grandmother. Definitely the men I owe money. They have real guns, Alexandros. I'm doomed."

Alexandros leaned back in his chair, staring at the ceiling. "What were you thinking? You know not even your parents can protect you from something like this, right?"

"It wasn't supposed to be like this. Honest! If we'd known, I would've... I don't know... moved to Argentina or something."

"Vito, tell me everything you know. Where is Rose? Is she in danger?" Alexandros said, pulling a pad of paper and picking up a pen.

"No—I don't know—maybe?" Vito sounded unsure. "When the men came to collect the money I owed their boss, they found out about Rose—and that I knew her, and that she was dating a Kallistratos. They decided they could make some money on the side. I told them it was a bad idea, but they wouldn't listen to me. They—they threatened to kill me, Alexandros. I think they might really do it. They have Allegra, too. If they don't kill me, she will! I don't know what to do!"

Alexandros rubbed his brow as he tried to get information out of Vito that would be useful in finding his sister and Rose. It took another five minutes—and enough tangents about Vito's 'bad luck with women' and 'terrible investments' to fill a confessional booth—before Alexandros finally got the full story.

Apparently, what was a light, temporary hold of Rose had escalated into an actual kidnapping, because, in Vito's words, 'people just can't be trusted anymore'.

"You are aware," Alexandros said slowly, "that kidnapping— intentional or not—is a crime."

"That's why I'm calling you!" Vito said, his voice climbing in pitch. "I'm in over my head here. I need help—desperately. They're both here —Allegra and Rose. I'll do whatever I can to keep them safe until someone gets here. I swear on my mother's pasta recipe."

"You'd better," Alexandros said darkly.

"I'm not a monster, Alex. I mean, I like dogs. And children. Most children. And—"

Alexandros hung up before Vito could dig the hole any deeper.

He immediately called Theo. The moment his brother answered, Alexandros didn't bother with pleasantries.

"You're not going to like this," he said. "The Rossi siblings have made an even bigger mess than usual—and this time, it involves Rose."

Allegra was pacing like a caged cat, her hands fluttering toward her hair, her mouth moving in an endless mutter of complaints.

"We could just wait," she said finally, throwing her arms wide. "Vito said he would fix it."

Rose arched a brow. "Yeah, and Vito sounds like a real 'fix-it' kind of guy. I'm sure he's putting up missing posters for me right now."

Allegra scowled. "Well, what do you suggest, then?"

Rose tapped her chin. "Oh, I don't know. Maybe we can escape?" she suggested sarcastically.

The other woman stared at her as if she'd just suggested they sprout wings. "Escape. From a locked room. On the second floor."

"Yes," Rose replied in exasperation. "I've slid down from the catwalks on ropes loads of times in the theatre."

Allegra's expression twisted. "You… what? Never mind. If you haven't noticed, we don't have any rope."

"Yes, we do. We can use the curtains—and the sheets," Rose said, gesturing toward the gauzy drapes at the window. "We'll pretend we are Rapunzel—we'll tie the sheets and curtains together and climb down."

Allegra gave her a flat look. "You're insane."

Rose tilted her head. "Didn't you ever climb a tree when you were a kid?"

"Of course not. Ladies don't climb trees."

"Uh-huh." Rose crossed her arms. "Well, unless you want the other side of your face to look like you went twelve rounds with a hand-slapper, you might want to learn."

That shut Allegra up.

Rose ignored Allegra's whining as she stripped the curtains from the rod and Allegra yanked the bedding off the mattress until they had a pile of fabric. Rose knotted the sheets, testing each with a sharp tug. Allegra hesitated, then grudgingly joined, her manicured fingers fumbling.

"This never would have happened if either Alexandros or Theo had just married me or Gina," Allegra muttered.

Rose didn't look up. "Why is that so important?"

Allegra sniffed. "Because my parents are nearly bankrupt. We need money."

Rose paused mid-knot and stared at her. "And did you, Gina, or Vito ever think about—oh, I don't know—getting a job?"

Allegra stared back, horrified. "I don't want to work."

Rose rolled her eyes. "Yeah, I guessed that, but selling your body is obviously a job you don't mind doing."

Allegra's mouth dropped open. "I did not—"

"You and your sister are literally trying to seduce a man for his money. I'm pretty sure that counts as selling yourself," Rose deadpanned, tossing another knotted section toward the window.

"This is slander," Allegra huffed.

"Yeah, well sue me after you get out of jail," Rose shot back, giving the last knot a good yank. "Now help me get this out the window."

They shoved the window open, the balmy air rushing in. Rose fed the knotted curtain-rope out until it dangled against the wall. It swayed slightly in the breeze, looking far less sturdy than she would have liked.

"Are you sure this will hold?" Allegra asked, her voice edging toward panic.

Rose flashed her a crooked grin and tried to hide her own fear as she slid a leg over the ledge. "Nope. But it'll make for one hell of an exit."

# Nineteen

**Kallistratos Security Systems: Athens, Greece**

The facial recognition from the photo came back fast.

The man in Rose's background was a petty crook, but the car he leaned against was registered to Allegra Rossi.

Theo's pulse went from steady to a deep, pounding thrum. Heat surged up his spine as if someone had thrown open a furnace door.

His phone rang. Alexandros.

"I can't talk right now—"

"You're going to want to," his brother cut in. "I just got off the phone with Vito. He knows where Rose is being held."

The icy grip on Theo's chest tightened. "Go on."

Alexandros relayed the mess in clipped, measured bursts—Vito's gambling debts, Allegra's harebrained 'delay' scheme, that Rose was with Allegra right now. And the address.

By the time Theo ended the call, his breathing was slow, deliberate.

He was going to kill them. All of them. Family friends be damned.

Markos, who'd caught enough of the conversation to follow, was already moving. "Angel. Cole. Gear up. We meet at the chopper in ten. Sending coordinates now for the location of the targets."

Theo's voice was calm and controlled. "I'll alert local police en route. No warning— if whoever is holding her senses us coming, they'll move her."

Ten minutes later, Theo and Markos climbed into the helicopter in silence. Angel would pilot the aircraft while Cole co-piloted. The countryside blurred past in shades of dusty gold and deep green, but Theo's focus was pinpointed on the location ahead.

He contacted the local authorities, debriefing them on what had happened. The local Municipal Police Chief, Homerus, was already aware of Rose's abduction after a local discovered an unconscious man along the road. Homerus assured him they would have vehicles and men ready by the time they landed.

Twenty-five minutes later, the helicopter set down in a farmer's field. The house where Rose was being held was on the far end of the village, approximately fifteen minutes by car.

Theo exited the helicopter and strode forward to clasp Homerus's hand as the police chief approached. Both men wore grim expressions.

"Mr. Kallistratos. I appreciate your assistance in this. There are only myself and two others. The village is small, and we don't have much crime—certainly nothing like this," Homerus admitted in a gruff, apologetic tone.

Theo nodded in understanding. "My team and I are trained for hostage situations. I have the permissions to handle this," he said, motioning at Cole, Markos, and Angel. "We'll go in first and secure the house and the hostages."

"They are two women?" Homerus asked, his brow furrowed with worry.

"Yes."

Theo's clipped answer was pulled from him. His throat tightened as he remembered Dani's recent near-death experience. His brother's wife had nearly died at the hands of a vengeful ex-boyfriend who had stalked her. She had barely made it out alive. If he and his team had been even a few minutes later, she would have died.

He pushed the thought away, knowing that any distraction could jeopardize the mission. He rode with Homerus while the rest of the team divided up into the other two police vehicles.

Fifteen minutes later, they slipped through olive groves, police blocking curious villagers at a distance.

"Two men on the back. No sign of movement inside yet," Angel murmured.

"One in front," Cole said.

Theo's jaw flexed. "Markos, you cover the west. I'll take the east side."

He and Markos fanned out—quiet, coordinated. The front guard went down with a muffled grunt courtesy of Cole.

"Back sentries neutralized," Angel said.

"Show off," Cole muttered.

"See if you can enter without being seen," Theo instructed.

"Roger that," both men replied.

Theo rounded the corner toward the east of the property—

—and froze.

There, dangling halfway out a second-story window, was Rose.

Using curtains and bed linen.

As. A. Rope.

*Is she insane?*

Her hair was a glorious mess. Her jeans were ripped, her knuckles white as she clung to the makeshift rope. She was hissing as she stared upward.

"You're supposed to wrap it around your hand—no, your hand, Allegra!"

A second pair of legs—dressed in an expensive skirt rather than climbing gear—poked awkwardly out of the window above her. Allegra Rossi, clearly not a fan of heights, was clinging in terror to the makeshift curtain rope like it was a live electrical wire.

"I am wrapping it!" Allegra snapped back. "This is a terrible idea!"

"I told you to throw your shoes out. You can't climb in six-inch heels. Kick them off. Just don't hit me. I knew I should have made you go first!"

"Why?" Allegra demanded, glaring down over her shoulder.

"So if I fall, I'd have someone to land on," Rose snapped.

"Ha-ha," Allegra retorted, slipping several inches with a low cry before she closed her eyes and clung to the knotted material.

Theo pinched the bridge of his nose. "*Christos!* Markos, I need your help," he muttered under his breath.

Seconds later, Markos appeared at his side, his lips twitching when he saw where Theo was staring. "Want me to get them down?"

Theo's glare shut that down immediately. "I'll get Rose."

He sprinted forward into the open. "*Agápi mou…* are you trying to give me a heart attack?"

Rose stiffened, a surprised cry of delight escaping her as she whipped her head around to stare down at him. The relief on her face warred with embarrassment.

"Theo!"

Allegra, still clinging above, twisted to look. "Who is that?"

"That," Rose said sweetly, glancing up at Allegra, "is the cavalry."

Theo's jaw clenched, but his voice was pure steel. "Stay still. Both of you."

Theo looked up when Angel leaned out the bedroom window the two women were escaping from.

"Inside is neutralized. Cole's contacted the police. There was only one hostile inside."

Allegra tilted her head back. "If it is a snotty little runt wearing a black jacket, I hope you knocked him good," she snapped.

Angel chuckled. "Let's just say he'll have a bit of a headache when he wakes up."

Theo slung his weapon over his shoulder and reached up, gripping Rose around her waist once she had slid down far enough for him to reach her.

The moment her feet touched down, his hands skimmed over her like he had to memorize her all over again.

"You're insane," he said quietly.

"But you love me anyway," she countered, breathless.

He kissed her—quick, fierce—before looking up at Allegra, still dangling like an overpriced chandelier.

"You're on your own."

"Wait—what?! *Theo!* Don't leave me here!" Allegra wailed, distraught.

Markos sighed, stepped forward, and motioned his hand at Allegra, muttering about "the things I do."

As the police swept inside to secure the property, Theo kept Rose tucked against him, his hand possessive at the small of her back. He was still burning with fury—but she was here, alive, safe. And that, for now, was enough.

He was done taking chances with Rose.

The second they'd cleared the property, Theo instructed Angel to fly them straight to Syros, to his family's villa. He hadn't let go of her since—his arm anchored around her shoulders, as if loosening his grip might give fate a chance to steal her away again.

"How's Christian?" Rose asked as the helicopter cut across the blue expanse of the Aegean.

"Fine," Theo said, his voice gruff with stress and leftover adrenaline. "A little disgruntled about being caught off-guard, but he's made a full recovery."

She hesitated before asking, "What will happen to Allegra and Vito?"

His jaw worked. "Honestly, I don't care." Then, grudgingly when she elbowed him, "But the Rossi family has influence. They'll probably end up with a slap on the wrist. Vito wasn't there, he tried to stop the kidnapping, and he helped us find you. And Allegra was being held herself, so…" He exhaled slowly. "There'll be a large enough scandal to clip their wings for a while."

Rose shifted against him. "She told me her parents were almost bankrupt."

Theo scoffed. "The Rossi family is far from bankrupt. Apollo and Dorothea are well-invested. They just put their three adult children on a 'budget' after discovering their recent… massive spending spree." His tone sharpened. "This should be a wake-up call for all of them."

A soft smile curved Rose's lips. "Allegra wasn't so bad once you got to know her. She just needs different friends—and possibly different siblings."

Theo couldn't help the chuckle that escaped. Shaking his head, he bent to kiss the top of her hair. "Only you could find something good out of this."

But when he closed his eyes, the humor bled into something heavier. He couldn't help imagining if they'd been too late…

He shoved the thought away, fighting the shudder that still threatened to break free.

Forty minutes later, the helicopter settled on the villa's helipad. Theo helped Rose down, his hand firm at her waist. He raised a hand to

Angel in thanks, knowing the man would return to pick up Markos and Cole, who had stayed behind to debrief Homerus.

They walked slowly through the garden, the patio tiles smooth underfoot, the air rich with the scent of bougainvillea and salt from the nearby sea. Ahead, Alexandros, Dani, and their parents waited. One look at their faces—relief written in every line—and Theo's throat tightened. His fingers tightened around Rose's hand until his knuckles ached.

Dani descended the steps, one hand resting on her baby bump with Alexandros right behind her. She wrapped Rose in a warm hug, and within moments the two women were trading stories—Dani calling Rose's ordeal 'more like a Big Bang episode' as they laughed over Allegra's nail preservation efforts.

His mother threaded her arm through Rose's. "Are you hungry, dear?"

Theo barely registered their voices. The sharp press of his brother's arms around him brought him back.

"Glad it worked out," Alexandros murmured.

A shudder ran through Theo before he could stop it. "Me too," he said quietly. It was the truth—and also the understatement of his life.

"Come," Christos suggested from behind them, his deep voice even. "A quiet drink on the terrace before dinner might be nice. We have company. They wanted to give you a moment."

Theo nodded, walking toward the steps—only to slow as a new pair of figures emerged onto the terrace.

Lorenzo. Sophia.

Rose's soft, almost broken cry snapped his gaze to her. She had gone still ahead of him, her eyes locked on the elderly couple, tears shimmering.

When they opened their arms, she surged forward, and they enveloped her in an embrace that was pure, unconditional love.

Theo stood rooted where he was, his chest a battlefield. This reunion could take her from him. Lorenzo and Sophia had already lost so much; he could see it in the way they clung to her, their bodies trembling.

He clenched his fists at his sides. He would not lose her. Not to danger. Not to the Rossi family. Not even to the people who loved her as fiercely as he did.

She was his. And after today, he knew he'd do anything—*anything*—to keep it that way.

The night air was warm but edged with a touch of coolness. This evening, the sea's breath met the shore in a symphony of hushed, whispering waves. Not loud and crashing, but soothing and gentle, like a soft caress.

Theo stood at the terrace rail, a glass of whiskey in hand, watching the moonlight ripple across the water. Dinner had been... lively. Rose had retired early with a wry smile and the comment that "being kidnapped takes a lot out of a girl." Dani had laughed and replied that being pregnant was just as bad.

Now, the villa was quiet.

He should have gone with Rose, but his emotions still rode too close to the surface. The thought of losing her had carved a hollow in his chest, and he needed a moment to fill it with something steadier before he saw her again.

Footsteps echoed softly against the tile behind him.

He turned, his gaze landing on Lorenzo. His godfather moved to stand beside him at the rail, the older man's presence grounding and familiar. They stood in companionable silence for a long moment, both staring out at the endless stretch of dark water.

"I've been following what's been going on," Lorenzo said finally, his voice low.

Theo frowned. "What do you mean?"

"After the DNA results came back, I shared them with Sophia, Lucinda, and Raff. I asked Raff to keep an eye on Rose." Lorenzo's gaze stayed on the water, but there was nothing casual in his tone. "I know about your relationship with my granddaughter."

Theo's lips twitched. Of course he knew. Lorenzo always knew.

"What are your intentions?"

Theo breathed out a sigh, the corners of his mouth lifting into a quiet chuckle. He looked down at the amber in his glass, swirling it once before lifting his gaze to meet Lorenzo's.

"I should have known you'd be on top of things." He let the truth come without hesitation. "I'm in love with her. And I'm going to ask her to marry me."

Lorenzo's face softened, a slow, genuine smile breaking across it. "Then you have my blessing. I would be proud to call you my son— not that I don't already think of you as one."

Something in Theo's chest loosened. The approval meant more than he'd realized, settling in his bones like a promise kept.

Lorenzo glanced toward the villa, his expression turning warm. "Sophia and Lucinda will work with your mother to plan the wedding. It will be a true joining of two great families."

Theo's lips curved. "God help me," he murmured, but there was no mistaking the quiet joy in his voice.

Lorenzo's chuckle was deep and satisfied as he lifted his own glass. "To you and Rose. And to the future. Thank you for bringing my family peace, Theo."

Theo raised his glass in return, the clink ringing softly between them. "To the future. To family."

The whiskey burned warm down his throat, but it was nothing compared to the heat of relief and anticipation in his chest.

For the first time since that phone call from Nikos, the knot in his stomach eased. Rose was safe. She was his. And now—finally—he could start thinking about forever.

The villa was quiet when Theo slipped back inside. The air carried the faint scent of sea and jasmine, a reminder of where they were... and that they'd made it here together.

In their room, the lamplight was low, casting a warm glow over the bed where Rose lay curled beneath the covers. He stood for a moment just watching her, letting the sight of her—safe, breathing, here—wash over him like a tide.

He crossed to the bathroom, stripped, then stepped into the shower. The rush of warm water beat against his tense muscles. He let it run over his face, down his neck, across his chest—that still felt tight from the hours he'd spent imagining losing her. By the time he turned the water off, the tension had eased, but his need for her had grown.

Sliding between the sheets, he eased close, careful not to wake her—until she sighed, her hand tracing down his chest in a touch that was both tender and claiming. Her lips brushed his shoulder, lingering there, warm and real, grounding him because she was here.

"I missed you," she murmured, snuggling closer and sliding her hand down to wrap around his full shaft.

He turned his head toward her, and in that moment, whatever fragile leash he'd been holding on his emotions unraveled, leaving only the raw need to hold and love her.

He rolled toward her, gathering her into his arms and kissing her like he needed her breath to survive. She kissed him back, her fingers curling into his hair and pulling him closer. The fear, the relief, the love —it all tangled together, fierce and overwhelming.

He cupped her face, brushing his thumb over the softness of her cheek as if committing her to memory—the curve of her lips, the warmth in her eyes, and the quiet strength that had kept her safe until he could reach her.

"I thought I lost you," he whispered against her mouth.

"You didn't," she murmured. "I'm right here."

His chest constricted. He kissed her again, slower this time, as if savoring each second, each taste. His hands moved over her with reverence, learning her all over again, mapping every inch as though proving to himself she was whole.

She bowed into him, her breathy gasps searing him. Her legs fell apart in invitation as her hips rose. The slick slide of flesh made him groan. He deepened his kiss, their tongues tangling in a wild dance.

When he finally slid into her, it wasn't with urgency but with a deep, steady connection—each movement a vow, each breath a silent promise he would never let her go.

She held him close, her legs curling around his waist, her breath soft in his ear. Their bodies moved together in a rhythm that felt older than either of them, unhurried and certain.

Her eyes found his in the lamplight, and whatever walls he'd built inside himself crumbled. He let her see everything—his fear, his devotion, the way she'd carved herself into him so deeply, there was no separating them.

"I love you, Rose. I love you so damn much, it terrifies me," he said, his voice rough, breaking just enough to betray the truth.

Her answering smile was tender, luminous. "I love you too."

He rolled his hips. His fingers threaded through her hair, tightening. He wanted to make love slowly, but his emotions were too ravaged, too close to the surface. She understood.

Her legs loosened from around his waist, her hands rising to cup his face, her gaze locking with his—wordless understanding passing between them.

"Love me, Theo. I don't want gentle. I want to know I'm alive… here… with you," she pleaded.

"God, Rose! *S'agapó*, my beautiful Rose. I love you, *kardiá mou.*"

He would love every inch of her body tonight. They both released a low moan when he pulled out of her. His lips worshipped her. He kissed his way down along her jaw to her throat. His lips pleasured her nipples until she was begging him for release.

He trailed down her smooth stomach and feasted. Her body writhed beneath the onslaught, but he held her there until she shattered.

While her body still trembled from her release, he guided her onto her stomach, lifting her onto her knees with a tenderness that contrasted the raw possession of his next thrust—burying himself fully, completely, as if staking his claim all over again.

"Theo!" she whimpered, sensitive to the point of pain.

"You're mine, Rose," he declared as he drove into her, wrapping his arms around her and cupping her breasts as he pulled her closer. He rocked his hips in deep thrusts, holding her tighter as he felt his release building. "And I'm yours."

"I… belong… to you," she choked, her voice cracking with emotion and need.

"Yes. Yes, *agápi mou!*" he shouted, his voice hoarse as he thrust one last time, burying himself as pleasure burst from him and his release filled her.

He stayed inside her, their bodies clinging as if parting was unthinkable. Each heartbeat, each breath, tethered him more tightly to her.

He wrapped his arms around her, his hand resting over her thundering heart like a guard. He continued to press tiny kisses to her hair and shoulder as she drifted to sleep against his chest, her breathing even and steady.

When he withdrew, still shuddering, he cleaned them both with quiet tenderness before curling back around her. She didn't wake.

His hand tenderly cupped her bare breast. Only then, with her soft and warm in his arms, did the restless beast inside him finally go still.

# Epilogue

Rose exhaled slowly, watching the sun spill golden light across the sand, the tide's edge catching it and turning to a shimmering ribbon.

The air was already warm but carried a salt-sweet breeze that curled through her hair, bringing with it the faint perfume of blooming jasmine from the villa gardens above.

Theo's hand stayed wrapped around hers as they walked, their bare feet sinking into cool, damp sand. The rhythmic hush of waves against the shore filled the spaces between their breaths, a steady heartbeat to the beginning of the day.

Rose took a deep breath, savoring the island's beauty and tranquility. She had been surprised when he had woken her early, pulling her from their bed. She had groaned and teasingly whined that it was too early, but he had tickled, then kissed her until she was breathless with need.

The morning held a quiet—the kind that seeped into your bones and made the world feel far away. But when he slowed, his grip tightening, she looked up to see his eyes on hers—intense, unwavering.

Without a word, he released her hand and lowered to one knee.

The sight punched the air from her lungs. This man—strong, infuriating, steady when everything else tilted—kneeling for her under the first rays of sunlight was almost too much for her heart to hold.

"Rose Smythe," he said, voice low and sure, though a thread of raw emotion ran through it, "I thought I knew what my life was. I thought I knew what I needed. Then you happened. You captivated me with one kiss. You promised me only one, but I knew even then that one would never be enough. Nothing has been the same since the night I saw you sitting there, alone at that table, sending every other man who came up scurrying for cover—thank God." He paused and drew in a deep, steadying breath. "You've scared me, made me laugh when I didn't think I could, and I fell in love so deeply it feels like my chest might burst trying to hold it in. I don't want a life that doesn't have you in it. Rose, will you do me the honor of marrying me?"

The velvet box opened in his palm, and the ring caught the sunlight—a sapphire the deep blue of the Aegean, wrapped in diamonds that caught the light like tiny stars.

Her throat tightened, and a choked laugh slipped through her tears like sunlight through rain. "You are ridiculously dramatic," she whispered, dropping to her knees in front of him. "Yes. Oh, Theo, yes. I would love to marry you. I love you."

When he slid the ring onto her finger, his hands lingered, warm and sure.

She was still crying when he leaned forward and drew her into his arms. His kiss filled her heart, chasing away every fear and doubt about whether they would make it. He was her Beast—and she loved him to the depths of her soul.

Laughing, she pulled away and wiped fruitlessly at her tears. The sound of clapping and catcalls from the terrace caused both of them to look up. She blushed, laughing as Alexandros, Dani, Theo's parents, and her grandparents stood looking down at them with huge smiles on their faces.

∼

Later that evening, dinner was anything but calm.

Sophia, Lucinda, and Theo's mother had commandeered the far end of the table, their chairs pulled tight together, their voices a musical mix of Greek and Italian. A color swatch book lay open between them, pale silks and deep velvets spilling like treasure onto the tablecloth. Someone had commandeered the bread basket as a pincushion for test arrangements of fabric, lace, and ribbon.

Rose had barely sat when Dani leaned over, eyes bright. "You know what it should be."

Rose groaned. "Dani…"

"A *Beauty and the Beast* theme," Dani declared, grinning. "You're Belle. And Theo—"

Across the table, Theo gave a long-suffering sigh as he envisioned them designing a replica of the stage ballroom. "Don't."

The glimmer in Dani's gaze said she already had the ballroom scene planned in her head.

Three days later, Theo wanted to groan and elope. He'd given his mother, Sophia, and Lucinda two weeks to plan the wedding. Rose had laughed and teased him about being impatient. He pointed out that it was mere minutes after the Beast turned human again that there was a wedding.

"How would you know that?" Alexandros asked with a confused expression. "I didn't know you were into romantic fairy tales."

"He came to the play at the theatre where I lived and worked," Rose said, reaching out to grasp his hand. "It's always been my favorite."

"Ah, that explains a lot, I think," Alexandros muttered.

"Sir, you have visitors," a servant announced.

"Who—"

His voice died when Apollo and Dorothea Rossi entered. Dorothea looked pale, Apollo drawn—both carrying a mix of embarrassment and fury that clung to them like a second skin.

The Rossi siblings entered behind their parents, subdued and dressed more conservatively than Theo could remember. Gina entered first, perfectly put-together despite the tension in her eyes. Allegra followed, her cream suit a sharp contrast to the guilt softening her expression. Vito trailed them, sporting a black eye and bruised chin, looking like he hadn't slept in a week.

They hovered in the doorway until Apollo waved them forward, the air charged with awkward anticipation.

"Theo, my children have something to say to you, your fiancée, and your family," Apollo said, his voice deep and commanding.

"I'm sorry," Gina muttered.

"Speak up, girl," Apollo snapped.

Gina pursed her lips. Theo was surprised when instead of resentment, he saw tears of remorse threatening to fall. Gina cleared her throat and spoke again, clearer this time.

"I'm sorry for being a brat to you and Alexandros. I—Daddy—" Gina started to whine, turning to her father.

"You can say your apologies to your mother and me later," Apollo snapped.

Gina sniffed and wiped at her cheek. "I shouldn't have behaved the way I did. It was un- unfitting, and- and I won't do it again," she choked out.

"It's Rose you owe the apology to, not me," Theo bit out, unmoved by Gina's tears.

"Theo—" Rose chided. "I forgive you."

"Thank you," Gina replied in a hoarse voice.

"Vito," Apollo ordered with a nod of his head.

Vito stepped forward, glanced at Alexandros, then Dani, and winced. He drew in a deep breath.

"I'm sorry I locked Dani in your stateroom, but please remember if I hadn't, you never would have met."

"Vito—an apology," Dorothea demanded.

Vito grimaced and continued. "I'm sorry I talked Gina into climbing into your bathtub, Theo."

"Oh, dear heavens," Dorothea muttered, fanning herself.

If he hadn't wanted to kill Vito, Theo decided he could almost enjoy this moment of torturing the spoiled playboy.

"I'm also sorry I mentioned your girlfriend to my—associates. If it helps, their friends aren't too happy with me at the moment either," Vito muttered, lifting a hand to his face.

"You're lucky I didn't kill you, Vito. If you ever come near Rose or Dani again, I will," Theo replied in a voice low enough that only Vito could hear it.

Vito swallowed and paled. "I won't. I... think it best if I focus on getting my life straightened out," he said hoarsely, stepping back.

"Vito, you and Gina wait for us in the car," Apollo ordered.

"Yes, Daddy," Gina mumbled.

"Yes, Father," Vito said, hurrying to exit.

"Allegra," Apollo motioned to his oldest daughter.

Allegra looked at Theo before her eyes turned to Rose. There was almost a wistful expression in them before she lowered her lashes.

"I'm sorry—for everything. I was wrong. I know I was wrong and can never make it up. I-I want you to know I understand why you don't want to be friends with my sister, brother, and me. I-I hope you won't blame our parents. It's not their fault. We were the ones who made bad choices." Her gaze moved to Rose, and she stepped closer to smile at her.

"It's crazy, but I learned a lot about myself from this little stunt. It was actually... fun, hanging out a window with you. Maybe if I had made better choices, especially if I had a friend—if I had known someone like you earlier—I could have turned out to be a better person."

Rose reached out and cupped Allegra's trembling hands in hers. "It was pretty cool hanging out—literally—with you." Allegra chuckled and sniffed. "I'm getting married in a couple of weeks. I was wondering if you'd like to be one of my bridesmaids?"

Theo shook his head in disbelief—only Rose could turn a rival into a bridesmaid.

"I—you want me to be a bridesmaid—in your wedding?"

"Yeah. I mean, it's not like I have a long list of friends, but you were pretty cool," Rose said, grinning.

Allegra's mascara smudged as tears gathered, and she pulled her hands free to wipe at them with a self-conscious laugh. "Yes. I... yes. I'd love to be in your wedding."

Theo caught Rose's hand and pulled her back against him. He kissed her temple, his body shaking with laughter. Only his beautiful Rose could tame a Beast more cursed than him.

Wedding preparations took over the villa in the days that followed—yards of fabric draped over sofas, flowers spilled from buckets in the kitchen, and the air was scented with lavender, roses, and coffee.

Amidst the chaos, Rose finally found a moment with Sophia and Lorenzo out on the terrace. An outdoor fire burned low, casting a warm amber glow across polished tile and palms.

She carried a box of photos she'd left untouched since her grandfather's death—too raw then to face, too full of ghosts.

Lorenzo set a worn photograph on the low table next to him. It was of a young woman with Rose's hair and face. Her mother, smiling wide in black and white.

"This came to me a few months ago," Lorenzo said, his voice quiet but steady. "I believe it was sent after your grandfather's death. From him… or his attorney. We never knew about you, Rose. And we never knew she'd married your father."

Sophia's hand slid into hers, warm and sure. "Your mother was headstrong, but her heart… it was always in the right place. She wrote to us—so many letters—telling us all she was learning, how grateful she was for her life, but never about your father—or you."

Lorenzo's jaw worked. "I should have gone to her. Or brought her home. But life—"

"—gets in the way," Rose finished softly.

Sophia squeezed her hand. "Having you here… it gives me peace. Knowing she was truly loved… that's all I could ask for."

"You're right. It was my grandfather who sent it. I-I found this letter this morning." Tears that she'd hoped she had finished shedding slid silently down her cheeks. "My grandfather had this box he kept special pictures and letters in. Most are love letters he sent my grandmother and pictures of her and my father when he was young. I wasn't ready to go through them after he died. I wanted to see if there were any pictures I could display at the wedding—so they could be here with me… and that's when I found this."

She held out the letter she had read over and over since she had found it earlier this morning. Theo had found her sobbing uncontrollably, and he held her and made love to her with a gentle passion that had her falling in love with him all over again.

Lorenzo took the letter from her and began reading.

*My dearest Rose,*

*They say that life is created in acts. The first act of my life was finding your grandmother and loving her. She might have been tiny, but she was powerful, and I loved her with every fiber of my being.*

*The second act of my life was when we had your father. It wasn't easy. I nearly lost your grandmother and Chris that cold November morning. I swore that if God let them survive, I'd never complain again. We had twenty beautiful years with him before—well, before. It nearly broke your grandma, and when she asked me to keep you, I couldn't tell her no, especially after we discovered your mother never told her parents about you.*

*The third act of my life was the most brilliant—because I had you. It was selfish and wrong, but you were my Rose, and I couldn't imagine life without you. But, in my selfishness, I didn't think about what would happen when I was gone—and you were all alone. When I found the photo your mom was going to send to her parents, in an envelope written by her, hidden among your grandmother's cards, I knew it was a sign. A sign that you might find the place where you belonged.*

*I'm with your grandmother and your dad now, but my heart will always be with you. We're watching over you. I hope you can one day forgive an old woman and an old man for wanting to keep you locked in a tower. Find the play that will enchant you, Princess. Find the Beast to your Belle, and live a wonderful, magical life. Because you are our beautiful little Rose.*

*Love, Pop*

Her shoulders shook, and her sobs were not the only ones in the room. She felt a comforting hand on her shoulder and knew it was Theo. She rose from her seat and hugged Lorenzo and Sophia.

"Livia knew we would find you when the time was right. She knew— and made sure we did," Sophia said in a trembling voice.

The night before the wedding, the villa was strung with lanterns swaying in the sea breeze, casting shifting patterns across the terrace tiles. The murmur of voices drifted from the dining room, but out here the world was hushed, the sea's slow breathing the only sound.

Theo stood at the railing, his arm around her, the salt air tangling their hair.

"Do you realize," Rose murmured, tracing the line of his shirt buttons with one finger, "that if we take a honeymoon in my van, we could disappear for weeks?"

Theo's lips curved against her temple. "We could."

"There're loads of places we didn't get to see: Carlsbad Caverns, the Painted Desert… Maybe… when we get back…" her voice tilted into teasing, though her eyes gleamed, "…well, I was thinking it might be kinda cool if Dani and Alexandros's son had a cousin around the same age to play with."

He tilted her chin up so he could capture her lips in an intense kiss. Her knees felt weak by the time he released her, and his eyes held a promise that he was ready to start creating a baby right then and there.

"I suggest," he murmured, "that we make sure there are lots of opportunities for you to get pregnant."

"Oh, yes. We'll need to do it a lot more than once," she whispered, sliding her tongue along his lower lip.

"Kiss me, Rose," he murmured, lifting her into his arms. "And never let me go."

As his kiss deepened, Rose knew her prince had discovered a way to tame her thorns without damaging the wild rose that bloomed only for him.

Love contemporary romances?
*The Girls From the Street* series has five amazing books and connects to
two other series!

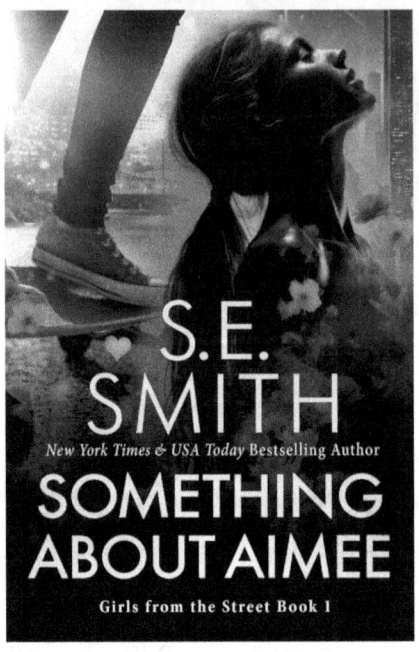

She was born on the streets; he was born to rule...

Sheikh Qadir Saif-Ad-Din understands the power behind money and
royalty, and he knows how to wield it, but when he is first dismissed
and then saved by a woman in tattered jeans carrying a skateboard, he
doesn't know what to think—except that he wants her!

Aimee is a street-smart free spirit who has always kept herself alive.
Through knives and guns and freezing cold, she has lived. But now
that she has saved a sheikh from assassination—and most dangerous
of all, they have fallen in love—the rules have changed, and this time it
will take more to stay alive, perhaps more than she can give.

# Additional Books

If you loved this story by me (Susan aka S.E. Smith), please leave a review! My websites are https://sesmithfl.com and https://sesmithya.com. Be sure to sign up for my newsletter to hear about new releases. Find your favorite way to keep in touch here: https://sesmithfl.com/contact-me/

RECOMMENDED READING ORDER LISTS:

https://sesmithfl.com/reading-list-by-events/

https://sesmithfl.com/reading-list-by-series/

RELATED SERIES:

Be on the lookout for RITA from the COSMOS' GATEWAY series, Rune and Dalla from the SECOND CHANCE series, and Harlem from the GIRLS FROM THE STREET series!

Also know that the DRAGON LORDS OF VALDIER universe now includes the CURIZAN WARRIOR series, the MARASTIN DOW WARRIORS series, the SARAFIN WARRIORS series, the DRAGONLINGS OF VALDIER series, A SEVEN KINGDOMS TALE, CYBORG PROTECTION UNIT, and the ZION WARRIORS series!

And keep an eye out for references of THE ALLIANCE series in *Jarmen's Jane Doe* from the LORDS OF KASSIS series!

## Contemporary / Romance

GIRLS FROM THE STREET

*Street smart. Heart strong. Unstoppable. A heart-pounding, emotional series where ordinary women are recognized as extraordinary and love proves the strongest weapon of all.*

S.E. SMITH SIGNATURE ROMANCE

HEART AND SOUL SERIES: *Passion. Power. Heart.*

*Breathtaking settings. Unforgettable characters. Sizzling chemistry.*

## Science Fiction / Romance

DRAGON LORDS OF VALDIER

It all started with a king who crashed on Earth, desperately hurt. He inadvertently discovered a species that would save his own.

## CURIZAN WARRIOR

The Curizans have a secret, kept even from their closest allies, but even they are not immune to the draw of a little known species from an isolated planet called Earth.

## MARASTIN DOW WARRIORS

The Marastin Dow are reviled and feared for their ruthlessness, but not all want to live a life of murder. Some wait for just the right time to escape....

## SARAFIN WARRIORS

A hilariously ridiculous human family who happen to be quite formidable... and a secret hidden on Earth. The origin of the Sarafin species is more than it seems. Those cat-shifting aliens won't know what hit them!

## DRAGONLINGS OF VALDIER

The Valdier, Sarafin, and Curizan Lords had children who just cannot stop getting into trouble! There is nothing as cute or funny as magical, shapeshifting kids, and nothing as heartwarming as family.

## COSMOS' GATEWAY

Cosmos created a portal between his lab and the warriors of Prime. Discover new worlds, new species, and outrageous adventures as secrets are unraveled and bridges are crossed.

## THE ALLIANCE

When Earth received its first visitors from space, the planet was thrown into a panicked chaos. The Trivators came to bring Earth into the Alliance of Star Systems, but now they must take control to prevent the humans from destroying themselves. No one was prepared for how the humans will affect the Trivators, though, starting with a family of three sisters....

## LORDS OF KASSIS

It began with a random abduction and a stowaway, and yet, somehow, the Kassisans knew the humans were coming long before now. The fate of more than one world hangs in the balance, and time is not always linear....

## ZION WARRIORS

*Time travel, epic heroics, and love beyond measure. Sci-fi adventures with heart and soul, laughter, and awe-inspiring discovery...*

## CYBORG PROTECTION UNIT

*On the Zion homeworld, an elite unit of enhanced warriors—part human, part machine—are charged with protecting their people from threats too dangerous for ordinary soldiers.*

## RINGS OF POWER

*Powerful mages. Epic love. Every world holds a new chance to rewrite destiny.*

### Paranormal / Fantasy / Romance

## MAGIC, NEW MEXICO

*Within New Mexico is a small town named Magic, an... unusual town, to say the least. With no beginning and no end, spanning genres, authors, and universes, hilarity and drama combine to keep you on the edge of your seat!*

## SPIRIT PASS

*There is a physical connection between two times. Follow the stories of those who travel back and forth. These westerns are as wild as they come!*

## SECOND CHANCE

*Stand-alone worlds featuring a woman who remembers her own death. Fiery and mysterious, these books will steal your heart.*

## MORE THAN HUMAN

*Long ago there was a war on Earth between shifters and humans. Humans lost, and today they know they will become extinct if something is not done....*

## THE FAIRY TALE SERIES

*A twist on your favorite fairy tales!*

## A SEVEN KINGDOMS TALE

*Long ago, a strange entity came to the Seven Kingdoms to conquer and feed on their life force. It found a host, and she battled it within her body for centuries while destruction and devastation surrounded her. Our story begins when the end is near, and a portal is opened....*

### Epic Science Fiction / Action Thrillers

## PROJECT GLIESE 581G

*An international team leave Earth to investigate a mysterious object in our solar system that was clearly made by someone, someone who isn't from Earth. Discover new worlds and conflicts in a sci-fi adventure sure to become your favorite!*

### New Adult / Young Adult

## BREAKING FREE

*A journey that will challenge everything she has ever believed about herself as danger reveals itself in sudden, heart-stopping moments.*

## THE DUST SERIES

*Fragments of a comet hit Earth, and Dust wakes to discover the world as he knew it is gone. It isn't the only thing that has changed, though, so has Dust…*

# About the Author

S.E. Smith is an *internationally acclaimed, New York Times* **and** *USA TODAY Bestselling* author of science fiction, romance, fantasy, paranormal, and contemporary works for adults, young adults, and children. She enjoys writing a wide variety of genres that pull her readers into worlds that take them away.